PENGUIN BOOK

T0200770

OF MICE AND

Born in Salinas, California, in 1902, JOHN STEINBECK grew up in a fertile agricultural valley about twenty-five miles from the Pacific Coast—and both valley and coast would serve as settings for some of his best fiction. In 1919 he went to Stanford University, where he intermittently enrolled in literature and writing courses until he left in 1925 without taking a degree. During the next five years he supported himself as a laborer and journalist in New York City and then as a caretaker for a Lake Tahoe estate, all the time working on his first novel, *Cup of Gold* (1929). After marriage and a move to Pacific Grove, he published two California fictions, *The Pastures of Heaven* (1932) and *To a God Unknown* (1933), and worked on short stories later collected in *The Long Valley* (1938). Popular success and financial security came only with *Tortilla Flat* (1935), stories about Monterey's paisanos. A ceaseless experimenter throughout his career, Steinbeck changed courses regularly. Three powerful novels of the late 1930s focused on the California laboring class: *In Dubious Battle* (1936), *Of Mice and Men* (1937), and the book considered by many his finest, *The Grapes of Wrath* (1939). Early in the 1940s, Steinbeck became a filmmaker with *The Forgotten Village* (1941) and a serious student of marine biology with *Sea of Cortez*. He devoted his services to the war, writing *Bombs Away* (1942) and the controversial play-novelette *The Moon Is Down* (1942). *Cannery Row* (1945), *The Wayward Bus* (1947), *The Pearl* (1947), *A Russian Journal* (1948), another experimental drama, *Burning Bright* (1950), and *The Log from the* Sea of Cortez (1951) preceded publication of the monumental *East of Eden* (1952), an ambitious saga of the Salinas Valley and his own family's history. The last decades of his life were spent in New York City and Sag Harbor with his third wife, with whom he traveled widely. Later books include *Sweet Thursday* (1954), *The Short Reign of Pippin IV: A Fabrication* (1957), *Once There Was a War* (1958), *The Winter of Our Discontent* (1961), *Travels with Charley in Search of America* (1962), *America and Americans* (1966), and the posthumously published *Journal of a Novel: The* East of Eden *Letters* (1969), *Viva Zapata!* (1975), *The Acts of King Arthur and His Noble Knights* (1976), and *Working Days: The Journals of* The Grapes of Wrath (1989). He died in 1968, having won a Nobel Prize in 1962.

BY JOHN STEINBECK

FICTION

Cup of Gold	The Moon Is Down
The Pastures of Heaven	Cannery Row
To a God Unknown	The Wayward Bus
Tortilla Flat	The Pearl
In Dubious Battle	Burning Bright
Saint Katy the Virgin	East of Eden
Of Mice and Men	Sweet Thursday
The Red Pony	The Winter of Our Discontent
The Long Valley	The Short Reign of Pippin IV

The Grapes of Wrath
Las uvas de la ira (Spanish-language edition of *The Grapes of Wrath*)
The Acts of King Arthur and His Noble Knights

NONFICTION

Sea of Cortez: A Leisurely Journal of Travel and Research
(in collaboration with Edward F. Ricketts)
Bombs Away: The Story of a Bomber Team
A Russian Journal *(with pictures by Robert Capa)*
The Log from the *Sea of Cortez*
Once There Was a War
Travels with Charley in Search of America
America and Americans
Journal of a Novel: The *East of Eden* Letters
Working Days: The Journals of *The Grapes of Wrath*

PLAYS

Of Mice and Men
The Moon Is Down

COLLECTIONS

The Portable Steinbeck
The Short Novels of John Steinbeck
Steinbeck: A Life in Letters

OTHER WORKS

The Forgotten Village (documentary)
Zapata (includes the screenplay of *Viva Zapata!*)

CRITICAL LIBRARY EDITION

The Grapes of Wrath (edited by Peter Lisca)

Of Mice and Men

A PLAY IN THREE ACTS

by John Steinbeck

PENGUIN BOOKS

PENGUIN BOOKS

Published by the Penguin Group
Penguin Group (USA) Inc., 375 Hudson Street, New York, New York 10014, U.S.A.
Penguin Group (Canada), 90 Eglinton Avenue East, Suite 700, Toronto,
Ontario, Canada M4P 2Y3 (a division of Pearson Penguin Canada Inc.)
Penguin Books Ltd, 80 Strand, London WC2R 0RL, England
Penguin Ireland, 25 St Stephen's Green, Dublin 2, Ireland
(a division of Penguin Books Ltd)
Penguin Group (Australia), 250 Camberwell Road, Camberwell, Victoria 3124,
Australia (a division of Pearson Australia Group Pty Ltd)
Penguin Books India Pvt Ltd, 11 Community Centre, Panchsheel Park,
New Delhi – 110 017, India
Penguin Group (NZ), 67 Apollo Drive, Rosedale, North Shore 0632,
New Zealand (a division of Pearson New Zealand Ltd)
Penguin Books (South Africa) (Pty) Ltd, 24 Sturdee Avenue,
Rosebank, Johannesburg 2196, South Africa
Penguin Books Ltd, Registered Offices: 80 Strand, London WC2R 0RL, England

First published in the United States of America by The Viking Press 1937
Published in Penguin Books 2009

ISBN 978-0-14-311720-9

Printed in the United States of America

PERSONS IN THE PLAY

GEORGE	*A small, sharp-faced ranch hand*
LENNIE	*His huge, but not bright, companion*
SLIM	*A jerk-line skinner, a master workman*
CANDY	*An old swamper*
THE BOSS	*Superintendent of the ranch*
CURLEY ·	*The boss's son*
CURLEY'S WIFE	
CARLSON	*A ranch hand*
WHIT	*A ranch hand*
CROOKS	*A negro stable buck*

CAST OF CHARACTERS

This play was first presented by Sam H. Harris at the Music Box Theatre on the evening of November 23, 1937, with the following cast:

GEORGE	*Wallace Ford*
LENNIE	*Broderick Crawford*
CANDY	*John F. Hamilton*
THE BOSS	*Thomas Findlay*
CURLEY	*Sam Byrd*
CURLEY'S WIFE	*Claire Luce*
SLIM	*Will Geer*
CARLSON	*Charles Slattery*
WHIT	*Walter Baldwin*
CROOKS	*Leigh Whipper*

Staged by George S. Kaufman
Settings by Donald Oenslager

SYNOPSIS OF SCENES

ACT ONE

SCENE I: A sandy bank of the Salinas River.
           Thursday night.

SCENE II: The interior of a bunkhouse.
           Late Friday morning.

ACT TWO

SCENE I: The same as Act I, Scene II.
           About seven-thirty Friday evening.

SCENE II: The room of the stable buck, a lean-to.
           Ten o'clock Saturday evening.

ACT THREE

SCENE I: One end of a great barn.
           Mid-afternoon, Sunday.

SCENE II: Same as Act I, Scene I.
           Sunday night.

TIME: The present.

PLACE: An agricultural valley in Northern California.

ACT ONE

ACT ONE: SCENE I

Thursday night.

A sandy bank of the Salinas River sheltered with willows—one giant sycamore right, upstage.

The stage is covered with dry leaves. The feeling of the stage is sheltered and quiet.

Stage is lit by a setting sun.

Curtain rises on an empty stage. A sparrow is singing. There is a distant sound of ranch dogs barking aimlessly and one clear quail call. The quail call turns to a warning call and there is a beat of the flock's wings. Two figures are seen entering the stage in single file, with George, the short man, coming in ahead of Lennie. Both men are carrying blanket rolls. They approach the water. The small man throws down his blanket roll, the large man follows and then falls down and drinks from the river, snorting as he drinks.

GEORGE

irritably: Lennie, for God's sake, don't drink so much.

Leans over and shakes Lennie. Lennie, you hear me! You gonna be sick like you was last night.

LENNIE

dips his whole head under, hat and all. As he sits upon the bank, his hat drips down the back: That's good. You drink some, George. You drink some too.

GEORGE

kneeling and dipping his finger in the water: I ain't sure it's good water. Looks kinda scummy to me.

LENNIE

imitates, dipping his finger also: Look at them wrinkles in the water, George. Look what I done.

GEORGE

drinking from his cupped palm: Tastes all right. Don't seem to be runnin' much, though. Lennie, you oughtn' to drink water when it ain't running. *Hopelessly:* You'd drink water out of a gutter if you was thirsty. *He throws a scoop of water into his face and rubs it around with his hand, pushes himself back and embraces his knees. Lennie, after watching him, imitates him in every detail.*

GEORGE

beginning tiredly and growing angry as he speaks: God damn it, we could just as well of rode clear to the ranch. That bus driver didn't know what he was talkin' about. "Just a little stretch down the highway," he says. "Just a little stretch"—damn near four miles. I bet he didn't want to stop at the ranch gate. . . . I bet he's too damn lazy to pull up. Wonder he ain't too lazy to stop at Soledad at all! *Mumbling:* Just a little stretch down the road.

LENNIE

timidly: George?

GEORGE:

Yeh . . . what you want?

LENNIE:

Where we goin', George?

GEORGE

jerks down his hat furiously: So you forgot that already, did you? So I got to tell you again! Jeez, you're a crazy bastard!

LENNIE

softly: I forgot. I tried not to forget, honest to God, I did!

GEORGE:

Okay, okay, I'll tell you again. . . . *With sarcasm:* I ain't got nothin' to do. Might just as well spen' all my

time tellin' you things. You forgit 'em and I tell you
again.

LENNIE

continuing on from his last speech: I tried and tried,
but it didn't do no good. I remember about the rabbits,
George!

GEORGE:

The hell with the rabbits! You can't remember nothing but them rabbits. You remember settin' in that
gutter on Howard Street and watchin' that black-
board?

LENNIE

delightedly: Oh, sure! I remember that . . . but . . .
wha'd we do then? I remember some girls come by,
and you says——

GEORGE:

The hell with what I says! You remember about us
goin' in Murray and Ready's and they give us work
cards and bus tickets?

LENNIE

confidently: Oh, sure, George . . . I remember that
now. *Puts his hand into his side coat-pocket; his con-
fidence vanishes. Very gently:* . . . George?

GEORGE:

Huh?

LENNIE

staring at the ground in despair: I ain't got mine. I musta lost it.

GEORGE:

You never had none. I got both of 'em here. Think I'd let you carry your own work card?

LENNIE

with tremendous relief: I thought I put it in my side pocket. *Puts his hand in his pocket again.*

GEORGE

looking sharply at him; and as he looks, Lennie brings his hand out of his pocket: Wha'd you take out of that pocket?

LENNIE

cleverly: Ain't a thing in my pocket.

GEORGE:

I know there ain't. You got it in your hand now. What you got in your hand?

LENNIE:

I ain't got nothing, George! Honest!

GEORGE:

Come on, give it here!

LENNIE

holds his closed hand away from George: It's on'y a mouse!

GEORGE:

A mouse? A live mouse?

LENNIE:

No . . . just a dead mouse. *Worriedly:* I didn't kill it. Honest. I found it. I found it dead.

GEORGE:

Give it here!

LENNIE:

Leave me have it, George.

GEORGE

sternly: Give it here! *Lennie reluctantly gives him the mouse.* What do you want of a dead mouse, anyway?

LENNIE

in a propositional tone: I was petting it with my thumb while we walked along.

GEORGE:

Well, you ain't pettin' no mice while you walk with me. Now let's see if you can remember where we're going. *George throws it across the water into the brush.*

16

LENNIE

looks startled and then in embarrassment hides his face against his knees: I forgot again.

GEORGE:

Jesus Christ! *resignedly:* Well, look, we are gonna work on a ranch like the one we come from up north.

LENNIE:

Up north?

GEORGE:

In Weed!

LENNIE:

Oh, sure I remember—in Weed.

GEORGE

still with exaggerated patience: That ranch we're goin' to is right down there about a quarter mile. We're gonna go in and see the boss.

LENNIE

repeats as a lesson: And see the boss!

GEORGE:

Now, look! I'll give him the work tickets, but you ain't gonna say a word. You're just gonna stand there and not say nothing.

Of Mice and Men

LENNIE:

Not say nothing!

GEORGE:

If he finds out what a crazy bastard you are, we won't get no job. But if he sees you work before he hears you talk, we're set. You got that?

LENNIE:

Sure, George . . . sure. I got that.

GEORGE:

Okay. Now when we go in to see the boss, what you gonna do?

LENNIE

concentrating: I . . . I . . . I ain't gonna say nothing . . . jus' gonna stand there.

GEORGE

greatly relieved: Good boy, that's swell! Now say that over two or three times so you sure won't forget it.

LENNIE

drones softly under his breath: I ain't gonna say nothing . . . I ain't gonna say nothing. . . . *Trails off into a whisper.*

GEORGE:

And you ain't gonna do no bad things like you done in Weed neither.

LENNIE

puzzled: Like I done in Weed?

GEORGE:

So you forgot that too, did you?

LENNIE

triumphantly: They run us out of Weed!

GEORGE

disgusted: Run us out, hell! We run! They was lookin' for us, but they didn't catch us.

LENNIE

happily: I didn't forget that, you bet.

GEORGE

lies back on the sand, crosses his hands under his head. And again Lennie imitates him: God, you're a lot of trouble! I could get along so easy and nice, if I didn't have you on my tail. I could live so easy!

LENNIE

hopefully: We gonna work on a ranch, George.

GEORGE:

All right, you got that. But we're gonna sleep here tonight, because . . . I want to. I want to sleep out. *The light is going fast, dropping into evening. A little wind whirls into the clearing and blows leaves A dog howls in the distance.*

LENNIE:

Why ain't we goin' on to the ranch to get some supper? They got supper at the ranch.

GEORGE:

No reason at all. I just like it here. Tomorrow we'll be goin' to work. I seen thrashing machines on the way down; that means we'll be buckin' grain bags. Bustin' a gut liftin' up them bags. Tonight I'm gonna lay right here an' look up! Tonight there ain't a grain bag or a boss in the world. Tonight, the drinks is on the . . . house. Nice house we got here, Lennie.

LENNIE

gets up on his knees and looks down at George, plaintively: Ain't we gonna have no supper?

GEORGE:

Sure we are. You gather up some dead willow sticks. I got three cans of beans in my bindle. I'll open 'em up while you get a fire ready. We'll eat 'em cold.

LENNIE

companionably: I like beans with ketchup.

GEORGE:

Well, we ain't got no ketchup. You go get wood, and don't you fool around none. Be dark before long. *Lennie lumbers to his feet and disappears into the brush. George gets out the bean cans, opens two of them, suddenly turns his head and listens. A little sound of splashing comes from the direction that Lennie has taken. George looks after him; shakes his head. Lennie comes back carrying a few small willow sticks in his hand.* All right, give me that mouse.

LENNIE

with elaborate pantomime of innocence: What, George? I ain't got no mouse.

GEORGE

holding out his hand: Come on! Give it to me! You ain't puttin' nothing over. *Lennie hesitates, backs away, turns and looks as if he were going to run. Coldly:* You gonna give me that mouse or do I have to take a sock at you?

LENNIE:

Give you what, George?

GEORGE:

You know goddamn well, what! I want that mouse!

LENNIE

almost in tears: I don't know why I can't keep it. It ain't nobody's mouse. I didn' steal it! I found it layin' right beside the road. *George snaps his fingers sharply, and Lennie lays the mouse in his hand.* I wasn't doin' nothing bad with it. Just stroking it. That ain't bad.

GEORGE

stands up and throws the mouse as far as he can into the brush, then he steps to the pool, and washes his hands: You crazy fool! Thought you could get away with it, didn't you? Don't you think I could see your feet was wet where you went in the water to get it? *Lennie whimpers like a puppy.* Blubbering like a baby. Jesus Christ, a big guy like you! *Lennie tries to control himself, but his lips quiver and his face works with an effort. George puts his hand on Lennie's shoulder for a moment.* Aw, Lennie, I ain't takin' it away just for meanness. That mouse ain't fresh. Besides, you broke it pettin' it. You get a mouse that's fresh and I'll let you keep it a little while.

LENNIE:

I don't know where there is no other mouse. I remember a lady used to give 'em to me. Ever' one she got she used to give it to me, but that lady ain't here no more.

GEORGE:

Lady, huh! . . . Give me them sticks there. . . . Don't even remember who that lady was. That was

22

your own Aunt Clara. She stopped givin' 'em to you.
You always killed 'em.

LENNIE

sadly and apologetically: They was so little. I'd pet
'em and pretty soon they bit my fingers and then I
pinched their head a little bit and then they was dead
. . . because they was so little. I wish we'd get the
rabbits pretty soon, George. They ain't so little.

GEORGE:

The hell with the rabbits! Come on, let's eat! *The light
has continued to go out of the scene so that when
George lights the fire, it is the major light on the
stage. George hands one of the open cans of beans to
Lennie.* There's enough beans for four men.

LENNIE

sitting on the other side of the fire, speaks patiently:
I like 'em with ketchup.

GEORGE

explodes: Well, we ain't got any. Whatever we ain't
got, that's what you want. God Almighty, if I was
alone, I could live so easy. I could go get a job of work
and no trouble. No mess . . . and when the end of
the month come, I could take my fifty bucks and go
into town and get whatever I want. Why, I could stay

23

in a cat-house all night. I could eat any place I want. Order any damn thing.

LENNIE

plaintively, but softly: I didn't want no ketchup.

GEORGE

continuing violently: I could do that every damn month. Get a gallon of whiskey or set in a pool room and play cards or shoot pool. *Lennie gets up to his knees and looks over the fire, with frightened face.* And what have I got? *Disgustedly:* I got *you.* You can't keep a job and you lose me every job I get!

LENNIE

in terror: I don't mean nothing, George.

GEORGE:

Just keep me shovin' all over the country all the time. And that ain't the worst—you get in trouble. You do bad things and I got to get you out. It ain't bad people that raises hell. It's dumb ones. *He shouts:* You crazy son-of-a-bitch, you keep me in hot water all the time. *Lennie is trying to stop George's flow of words with his hands. Sarcastically:* You just wanta feel that girl's dress. Just wanta pet it like it was a mouse. Well, how the hell'd she know you just wanta feel her dress?

24

How'd she know you'd just hold onto it like it was a mouse?

LENNIE

in a panic: I didn't mean to, George!

GEORGE:

Sure you didn't mean to. You didn't mean for her to yell bloody hell, either. You didn't mean for us to hide in the irrigation ditch all day with guys out lookin' for us with guns. Alla time it's something you didn't mean. God damn it, I wish I could put you in a cage with a million mice and let them pet *you*. *George's anger leaves him suddenly. For the first time he seems to see the expression of terror on Lennie's face. He looks down ashamedly at the fire, and maneuvers some beans onto the blade of his pocket-knife and puts them into his mouth.*

LENNIE

after a pause: George! *George purposely does not answer him.* George?

GEORGE:

What do you want?

LENNIE:

I was only foolin', George. I don't want no ketchup. I wouldn't eat no ketchup if it was right here beside me.

Of Mice and Men

GEORGE

with a sullenness of shame: If they was some here you could have it. And if I had a thousand bucks I'd buy ya a bunch of flowers.

LENNIE:

I wouldn't eat no ketchup, George. I'd leave it all for you. You could cover your beans so deep with it, and I wouldn't touch none of it.

GEORGE

refusing to give in from his sullenness, refusing to look at Lennie: When I think of the swell time I could have without you, I go nuts. I never git no peace!

LENNIE:

You want I should go away and leave you alone?

GEORGE:

Where the hell could you go?

LENNIE:

Well, I could . . . I could go off in the hills there. Some place I could find a cave.

GEORGE:

Yeah, how'd ya eat? You ain't got sense enough to find nothing to eat.

LENNIE:

I'd find things. I don't need no nice food with ketchup.

26

I'd lay out in the sun and nobody would hurt me. And if I found a mouse—why, I could keep it. Wouldn't nobody take it away from me.

GEORGE

at last he looks up: I been mean, ain't I?

LENNIE

presses his triumph: If you don't want me, I can go right in them hills, and find a cave. I can go away any time.

GEORGE:

No. Look! I was just foolin' ya. 'Course I want you to stay with me. Trouble with mice is you always kill 'em. *He pauses.* Tell you what I'll do, Lennie. First chance I get I'll find you a pup. Maybe you wouldn't kill it. That would be better than mice. You could pet it harder.

LENNIE

still avoiding being drawn in: If you don't want me, you only gotta say so. I'll go right up on them hills and live by myself. And I won't get no mice stole from me.

GEORGE:

I want you to stay with me. Jesus Christ, somebody'd

shoot you for a coyote if you was by yourself. Stay with me. Your Aunt Clara wouldn't like your runnin' off by yourself, even if she is dead.

LENNIE:

George?

GEORGE:

Huh?

LENNIE

craftily: Tell me—like you done before.

GEORGE:

Tell you what?

LENNIE:

About the rabbits.

GEORGE

near to anger again: You ain't gonna put nothing over on me!

LENNIE

pleading: Come on, George . . . tell me! Please! Like you done before.

GEORGE:

You get a kick out of that, don't you? All right, I'll tell you. And then we'll lay out our beds and eat our dinner.

28

LENNIE:

Go on, George.

Unrolls his bed and lies on his side, supporting his head on one hand. George lays out his bed and sits crosslegged on it. George repeats the next speech rhythmically, as though he had said it many times before.

GEORGE:

Guys like us that work on ranches is the loneliest guys in the world. They ain't got no family. They don't belong no place. They come to a ranch and work up a stake and then they go in to town and blow their stake. And then the first thing you know they're poundin' their tail on some other ranch. They ain't got nothin' to look ahead to.

LENNIE

delightedly: That's it, that's it! Now tell how it is with us.

GEORGE

still almost chanting: With us it ain't like that. We got a future. We got somebody to talk to that gives a damn about us. We don't have to sit in no barroom blowin' in our jack, just because we got no place else

29

to go. If them other guys gets in jail, they can rot for all anybody gives a damn.

LENNIE

who cannot restrain himself any longer. Bursts into speech: But not us! And why? Because . . . because I got you to look after me . . . and you got me to look after you . . . and that's why! *He laughs.* Go on, George!

GEORGE:

You got it by heart. You can do it yourself.

LENNIE:

No, no. I forget some of the stuff. Tell about how it's gonna be.

GEORGE:

Some other time.

LENNIE:

No, tell how it's gonna be!

GEORGE:

Okay. Some day we're gonna get the jack together and we're gonna have a little house, and a couple of acres and a cow and some pigs and . . .

LENNIE

shouting: And live off the fat of the land! And have rabbits. Go on, George! Tell about what we're gonna have in the garden. And about the rabbits in the cages. Tell about the rain in the winter . . . and about the stove and how thick the cream is on the milk, you can hardly cut it. Tell about that, George!

GEORGE:

Why don't you do it yourself—you know all of it!

LENNIE:

It ain't the same if I tell it. Go on now. How I get to tend the rabbits.

GEORGE

resignedly: Well, we'll have a big vegetable patch and a rabbit hutch and chickens. And when it rains in the winter we'll just say to hell with goin' to work. We'll build up a fire in the stove, and set around it and listen to the rain comin' down on the roof—Nuts! *Begins to eat with his knife.* I ain't got time for no more. *He falls to eating. Lennie imitates him, spilling a few beans from his mouth with every bite. George, gesturing with his knife:* What you gonna say tomorrow when the boss asks you questions?

LENNIE

stops chewing in the middle of a bite, swallows painfully. His face contorts with thought: I . . . I ain't gonna say a word.

31

GEORGE:

Good boy. That's fine. Say, maybe you're gittin' better. I bet I can let you tend the rabbits . . . specially if you remember as good as that!

LENNIE

choking with pride: I can remember, by God!

GEORGE

as though remembering something, points his knife at Lennie's chest: Lennie, I want you to look around here. Think you can remember this place? The ranch is 'bout a quarter mile up that way. Just follow the river and you can get here.

LENNIE

looking around carefully: Sure, I can remember here. Didn't I remember 'bout not gonna say a word?

GEORGE:

'Course you did. Well, look, Lennie, if you just happen to get in trouble, I want you to come right here and hide in the brush.

LENNIE

slowly: Hide in the brush.

GEORGE:

Hide in the brush until I come for you. Think you can remember that?

LENNIE:

Sure I can, George. Hide in the brush till you come for me!

GEORGE:

But you ain't gonna get in no trouble. Because if you do I won't let you tend the rabbits.

LENNIE:

I won't get in no trouble. I ain't gonna say a word.

GEORGE:

You got it. Anyways, I hope so. *George stretches out on his blankets. The light dies slowly out of the fire until only the faces of the two men can be seen. George is still eating from his can of beans.* It's gonna be nice sleeping here. Lookin' up . . . and the leaves . . . Don't build up no more fire. We'll let her die. Jesus, you feel free when you ain't got a job—if you ain't hungry.

They sit silently for a few moments. A night owl is heard far off. From across the river there comes the sound of a coyote howl and on the heels of the howl all the dogs in the country start to bark.

LENNIE

from almost complete darkness: George?

GEORGE:

What do you want?

LENNIE:

Let's have different color rabbits, George.

GEORGE:

Sure. Red rabbits and blue rabbits and green rabbits. Millions of 'em!

LENNIE:

Furry ones, George. Like I seen at the fair in Sacramento.

GEORGE:

Sure. Furry ones.

LENNIE:

'Cause I can jus' as well go away, George, and live in a cave.

GEORGE

amiably: Aw, shut up.

LENNIE

after a long pause: George?

GEORGE:

What is it?

LENNIE:

I'm shutting up, George. *A coyote howls again.*

CURTAIN

ACT ONE: SCENE II

Late Friday morning.

The interior of a bunkhouse.

Walls, white-washed board and bat. Floors unpainted.

There is a heavy square table with upended boxes around it used for chairs. Over each bunk there is a box nailed to the wall which serves as two shelves on which are the private possessions of the working men.

On top of each bunk there is a large noisy alarm clock ticking madly.

The sun is streaking through the windows. NOTE: *Articles in the boxes on wall are soap, talcum powder, razors, pulp magazines, medicine bottles, combs, and from nails on the sides of the boxes a few neckties.*

There is a hanging light from the ceiling over the table, with a round dim reflector on it.

The curtain rises on an empty stage. Only the ticking of the many alarm clocks is heard.

Candy, George and Lennie are first seen passing the open window of the bunkhouse.

CANDY:

This is the bunkhouse here. Door's around this side. *The latch on the door rises and Candy enters, a stoop-shouldered old man. He is dressed in blue jeans and a denim coat. He carries a big push broom in his left hand. His right hand is gone at the wrist. He grasps things with his right arm between arm and side. He walks into the room followed by George and Lennie. Conversationally:* The boss was expecting you last night. He was sore as hell when you wasn't here to go out this morning. *Points with his handless arm:* You can have them two beds there.

GEORGE:

I'll take the top one . . . I don't want you falling down on me. *Steps over to the bunk and throws his blankets down. He looks into the nearly empty box shelf over it, then picks up a small yellow can.* Say, what the hell's this?

CANDY:

I don' know.

GEORGE:

Says "positively kills lice, roaches and other scourges." What the hell kinda beds you givin' us, anyway? We don't want no pants rabbits.

CANDY

shifts his broom, holding it between his elbow and his side, takes the can in his left hand and studies the label carefully: Tell you what . . . last guy that had this bed was a blacksmith. Helluva nice fellow. Clean a guy as you'd want to meet. Used to wash his hands even *after* he et.

GEORGE

with gathering anger: Then how come he got pillow-pigeons? *Lennie puts his blankets on his bunk and sits down, watching George with his mouth slightly open.*

CANDY:

Tell you what. This here blacksmith, name of Whitey, was the kinda guy that would put that stuff around even if there wasn't no bugs. Tell you what he used to do. He'd peel *his* boiled potatoes and take out every little spot before he et it, and if there was a red splotch on an egg, he'd scrape it off. Finally quit about the food. That's the kind of guy Whitey was. Clean. Used to dress up Sundays even when he wasn't goin' no place. Put on a necktie even, and then set in the bunkhouse.

GEORGE

skeptically: I ain't so sure. What da' ya say he quit for?

CANDY

puts the can in his pocket, rubs his bristly white whiskers with his knuckles. Why . . . he just quit the way a guy will. Says it was the food. Didn't give no other reason. Just says "give me my time" one night, the way any guy would. *George lifts his bed tick and looks underneath, leans over and inspects the sacking carefully. Lennie does the same with his bed.*

GEORGE

half satisfied: Well, if there's any grey-backs in this bed, you're gonna hear from me! *He unrolls his blankets and puts his razor and bar of soap and comb and bottle of pills, his liniment and leather wristband in the box.*

CANDY:

I guess the boss'll be out here in a minute to write your name in. He sure was burned when you wasn't here this morning. Come right in when we was eatin' breakfast and says, "Where the hell's them new men?" He give the stable buck hell, too. Stable buck's a nigger.

GEORGE:

Nigger, huh!

CANDY:

Yeah. *Continues:* Nice fellow too. Got a crooked back

where a horse kicked him. Boss gives him hell when he's mad. But the stable buck don't give a damn about that.

GEORGE:

What kinda guy is the boss?

CANDY:

Well, he's a pretty nice fella for a boss. Gets mad sometimes. But he's pretty nice. Tell you what. Know what he done Christmas? Brung a gallon of whiskey right in here and says, "Drink hearty, boys, Christmas comes but once a year!"

GEORGE:

The hell he did! A whole gallon?

CANDY:

Yes, sir. Jesus, we had fun! They let the nigger come in that night. Well, sir, a little skinner name Smitty took after the nigger. Done pretty good too. The guys wouldn't let him use his feet so the nigger got him. If he could a used his feet Smitty says he would have killed the nigger. The guys says on account the nigger got a crooked back Smitty can't use his feet. *He smiles in reverie at the memory.*

GEORGE:

Boss the owner?

CANDY:

Naw! Superintendent. Big land company. . . . Yes, sir, that night . . . he come right in here with a whole gallon . . . he set right over there and says, "Drink hearty, boys," . . . he says. . . . *The door opens. Enter the Boss. He is a stocky man, dressed in blue jean trousers, flannel shirt, a black unbuttoned vest and a black coat. He wears a soiled brown Stetson hat, a pair of high-heeled boots and spurs. Ordinarily he puts his thumbs in his belt. Candy, shuffling towards the door, rubbing his whiskers with his knuckles as he goes:* Them guys just come. *Candy exits and shuts the door behind him.*

BOSS:

I wrote Murray and Ready I wanted two men this morning. You got your work slips?

GEORGE

digs in his pockets, produces two slips, and hands them to the Boss: Here they are.

BOSS

reading the slips: Well, I see it wasn't Murray and Ready's fault. It says right here on the slip, you was to be here for work this morning.

40

GEORGE:

Bus driver give us a bum steer. We had to walk ten miles. That bus driver says we was here when we wasn't. We couldn't thumb no rides. *George scowls meaningly at Lennie and Lennie nods to show that he understands.*

BOSS:

Well, I had to send out the grain teams short two buckers. It won't do any good to go out now until after dinner. You'd get lost. *Pulls out his time book, opens it to where a pencil is stuck between the leaves. Licks his pencil carefully.* What's your name?

GEORGE:

George Milton.

BOSS:

George Milton. *Writing:* And what's yours?

GEORGE:

His name's Lennie Small.

BOSS:

Lennie Small. *Writing:* Le's see, this is the twentieth. Noon the twentieth. . . . *Makes positive mark. Closes the book and puts it in his pocket.* Where you boys been workin'?

GEORGE:

Up around Weed.

BOSS

to Lennie: You too?

GEORGE:

Yeah. Him too.

BOSS

to Lennie: Say, you're a big fellow, ain't you?

GEORGE:

Yeah, he can work like hell, too.

BOSS:

He ain't much of a talker, though, is he?

GEORGE:

No, he ain't. But he's a hell of a good worker. Strong as a bull.

LENNIE

smiling: I'm strong as a bull. *George scowls at him and Lennie drops his head in shame at having forgotten.*

BOSS

sharply: You are, huh? What can you do?

GEORGE:

He can do anything.

42

BOSS

addressing Lennie: What can you do? *Lennie, looking at George, gives a high nervous chuckle.*

GEORGE

quickly: Anything you tell him. He's a good skinner. He can wrestle grain bags, drive a cultivator. He can do anything. Just give him a try.

BOSS:

turning to George: Then why don't you let *him* answer? *Lennie laughs.* What's he laughing about?

GEORGE:

He laughs when he gets excited.

BOSS

Yeah?

GEORGE

loudly: But he's a goddamn good worker. I ain't saying he's bright, because he ain't. But he can put up a four hundred pound bale.

BOSS:

hooking his thumbs in his belt: Say, what you sellin'?

GEORGE:

Huh?

BOSS:

I said what stake you got in this guy? You takin' his pay away from him?

GEORGE:

No. Of course I ain't!

BOSS

Yell, I never seen one guy take so much trouble for another guy. I just like to know what your percentage is.

GEORGE:

He's my . . . cousin. I told his ole lady I'd take care of him. He got kicked in the head by a horse when he was a kid. He's all right. . . . Just ain't bright. But he can do anything you tell him.

BOSS:

turning half away: Well, God knows he don't need no brains to buck barley bags. *He turns back.* But don't you try to put nothing over, Milton. I got my eye on you. Why'd you quit in Weed?

GEORGE

promptly: Job was done.

BOSS

What kind of job?

GEORGE:

Why . . . we was diggin' a cesspool.

44

BOSS:

after a pause: All right. But don't try to put nothing over 'cause you can't get away with nothing. I seen wise guys before. Go out with the grain teams after dinner. They're out pickin' up barley with the thrashin' machines. Go out with Slim's team.

GEORGE:

Slim?

BOSS:

Yeah. Big, tall skinner. You'll see him at dinner. *Up to this time the Boss has been full of business. He has been calm and suspicious. In the following lines he relaxes, but gradually, as though he wanted to talk but felt always the burden of his position. He turns toward the door, but hesitates and allows a little warmth into his manner.* Been on the road long?

GEORGE

obviously on guard: We was three days in 'Frisco lookin' at the boards.

BOSS:

with heavy jocularity: Didn't go to no night clubs, I 'spose?

GEORGE

stiffly: We was lookin' for a job.

BOSS:

attempting to be friendly: That's a great town if you got a little jack, Frisco.

GEORGE

refusing to be drawn in: We didn't have no jack for nothing like that.

BOSS:

realizes there is no contact to establish; grows rigid with his position again: Go out with the grain teams after dinner. When my hands work hard they get pie and when they loaf they bounce down the road on their can. You ask anybody about me. *He turns and walks out of bunkhouse.*

GEORGE

turns to Lennie: So you wasn't gonna say a word! You was gonna leave your big flapper shut. I was gonna do the talkin'. . . . You goddamn near lost us the job!

LENNIE

stares hopelessly at his hands: I forgot.

GEORGE:

You forgot. You always forget. Now, he's got his eye on us. Now, we gotta be careful and not make no slips. You keep your big flapper shut after this.

46

LENNIE:

He talked like a kinda nice guy towards the last.

GEORGE

angrily: He's the boss, ain't he? Well, he's the boss first an' a nice guy afterwards. Don't you have nothin' to do with no boss, except do your work and draw your pay. You can't never tell whether you're talkin' to the nice guy or the boss. Just keep your goddamn mouth shut. Then you're all right.

LENNIE:

George?

GEORGE:

What you want now?

LENNIE:

I wasn't kicked in the head with no horse, was I, George?

GEORGE:

Be a damn good thing if you was. Save everybody a hell of a lot of trouble!

LENNIE

flattered: You says I was your cousin.

GEORGE:

Well, that was a goddamn lie. And I'm glad it was. Why, if I was a relative of yours—— *He stops and lis-*

47

tens, then steps to the front door, and looks out. Say, what the hell you doin', listenin'?

CANDY

comes slowly into the room. By a rope, he leads an ancient drag-footed, blind sheep dog. Guides it from running into a table leg, with the rope. Sits down on a box, and presses the hind quarters of the old dog down. Naw . . . I wasn't listenin'. . . . I was just standin' in the shade a minute, scratchin' my dog. I jest now finished swamping out the washhouse.

GEORGE:

You was pokin' your big nose into our business! I don't like nosey guys.

CANDY

looks uneasily from George to Lennie and then back: I jest come there . . . I didn't hear nothing you guys was sayin'. I ain't interested in nothing you was sayin'. A guy on a ranch don't never listen. Nor he don't ast no questions.

GEORGE

slightly mollified: Damn right he don't! Not if the guy wants to stay workin' long. *His manner changes.* That's a helluva ole dog.

48

CANDY:

Yeah. I had him ever since he was a pup. God, he was a good sheep dog, when he was young. *Rubs his cheek with his knuckles.* How'd you like the boss?

GEORGE:

Pretty good! Seemed all right.

CANDY:

He's a nice fella. You got ta take him right, of course. He's runnin' this ranch. He don't take no nonsense.

GEORGE:

What time do we eat? Eleven-thirty? *Curley enters. He is dressed in working clothes. He wears brown high-heeled boots and has a glove on his left hand.*

CURLEY:

Seen my ole man?

CANDY:

He was here just a minute ago, Curley. Went over to the cookhouse, I think.

CURLEY:

I'll try to catch him. *Looking over at the new men, measuring them. Unconsciously bends his elbow and closes his hand and goes into a slight crouch. He walks gingerly close to Lennie.* You the new guys my ole man was waitin' for?

GEORGE:

Yeah. We just come in.

CURLEY:

How's it come you wasn't here this morning?

GEORGE:

Got off the bus too soon.

CURLEY

again addressing Lennie: My ole man got to get the grain out. Ever bucked barley?

GEORGE

quickly: Hell, yes. Done a lot of it.

CURLEY:

I mean him. *To Lennie:* Ever bucked barley?

GEORGE:

Sure he has.

CURLEY

irritatedly: Let the big guy talk!

GEORGE:

'Spose he don't want ta talk?

CURLEY

pugnaciously: By Christ, he's gotta talk when he's spoke to. What the hell you shovin' into this for?

GEORGE

stands up and speaks coldly: Him and me travel together.

50

CURLEY:

Oh, so it's that way?

GEORGE

tense and motionless: What way?

CURLEY

letting the subject drop: And you won't let the big guy talk? Is that it?

GEORGE:

He can talk if he wants to tell you anything. *He nods slightly to Lennie.*

LENNIE

in a frightened voice: We just come in.

CURLEY:

Well, next time you answer when you're spoke to, then.

GEORGE:

He didn't do nothing to you.

CURLEY

measuring him: You drawin' cards this hand?

GEORGE

quietly: I might.

CURLEY

stares at him for a moment, his threat moving to the future: I'll see you get a chance to ante, anyway. *He walks out of the room.*

GEORGE

after he has made his exit: Say, what the hell's he got on his shoulder? Lennie didn't say nothing to him.

CANDY

looks cautiously at the door: That's the boss's son. Curley's pretty handy. He done quite a bit in the ring. The guys say he's pretty handy.

GEORGE:

Well, let 'im be handy. He don't have to take after Lennie. Lennie didn't do nothing to him.

CANDY

considering: Well . . . tell you what, Curley's like a lot a little guys. He hates big guys. He's alla time pickin' scraps with big guys. Kinda like he's mad at 'em because *he* ain't a big guy. You seen little guys like that, ain't you—always scrappy?

GEORGE:

Sure, I seen plenty tough little guys. But this here Curley better not make no mistakes about Lennie. Lennie ain't handy, see, but this Curley punk's gonna get hurt if he messes around with Lennie.

CANDY

skeptically: Well, Curley's pretty handy. You know, it never did seem right to me. 'Spose Curley jumps a big guy and licks him. Everybody says what a game guy Curley is. Well, 'spose he jumps 'im and gits licked, everybody says the big guy oughta pick somebody his own size. Seems like Curley ain't givin' nobody a chance.

GEORGE

watching the door: Well, he better watch out for Lennie. Lennie ain't no fighter. But Lennie's strong and quick and Lennie don't know no rules. *Walks to the square table, and sits down on one of the boxes. Picks up scattered cards and pulls them together and shuffles them.*

CANDY:

Don't tell Curley I said none of this. He'd slough me! He jus' don't give a damn. Won't ever get canned because his ole man's the boss!

GEORGE

cuts the cards. Turns over and looks at each one as he throws it down: This guy Curley sounds like a son-of-a-bitch to me! I don't like mean little guys!

CANDY:

Seems to me like he's worse lately. He got married a couple of weeks ago. Wife lives over in the boss's house. Seems like Curley's worse'n ever since he got

53

married. Like he's settin' on a ant-hill an' a big red ant come up an' nipped 'im on the turnip. Just feels so goddamn miserable he'll strike at anything that moves. I'm kinda sorry for 'im.

GEORGE:

Maybe he's showin' off for his wife.

CANDY:

You seen that glove on his left hand?

GEORGE:

Sure I seen it!

CANDY:

Well, that glove's full of vaseline.

GEORGE:

Vaseline? What the hell for?

CANDY:

Curley says he's keepin' that hand soft for his wife.

GEORGE:

That's a dirty kind of a thing to tell around.

CANDY:

I ain't quite so sure. I seen such funny things a guy will do to try to be nice. I ain't sure. But you jus' wait till you see Curley's wife!

GEORGE

begins to lay out a solitaire hand, speaks casually: Is she purty?

CANDY:

Yeah. Purty, but——

GEORGE

studying his cards: But what?

CANDY:

Well, she got the eye.

GEORGE

still playing at his solitaire hand: Yeah? Married two weeks an' got the eye? Maybe that's why Curley's pants is fulla ants.

CANDY:

Yes, sir, I seen her give Slim the eye. Slim's a jerk-line skinner. Hell of a nice fella. Well, I seen her give Slim the eye. Curley never seen it. And I seen her give a skinner named Carlson the eye.

GEORGE

pretending a very mild interest: Looks like we was gonna have fun!

CANDY

stands up: Know what I think? *Waits for an answer. George doesn't answer.* Well, I think Curley's married himself a tart.

GEORGE

casually: He ain't the first. Black queen on a red king. Yes, sir . . . there's plenty done that!

CANDY

moves towards the door, leading his dog out with him:
I got to be settin' out the wash basins for the guys.
The teams'll be in before long. You guys gonna buck
barley?

GEORGE:

Yeah.

CANDY:

You won't tell Curley nothing I said?

GEORGE:

Hell, no!

CANDY

just before he goes out the door, he turns back: Well,
you look her over, mister. You see if she ain't a tart!
He exits.

GEORGE

continuing to play out his solitaire. He turns to Lennie:
Look, Lennie, this here ain't no set-up. You gonna
have trouble with that Curley guy. I seen that kind
before. You know what he's doin'. He's kinda feelin'
you out. He figures he's got you scared. And he's gonna
take a sock at you, first chance he gets.

LENNIE

frightened: I don't want no trouble. Don't let him sock
me, George!

56

GEORGE:

I hate them kind of bastards. I seen plenty of 'em. Like the ole guy says: "Curley don't take no chances. He always figures to win." *Thinks for a moment.* If he tangles with you, Lennie, we're goin' get the can. Don't make no mistake about that. He's the boss's kid. Look, you try to keep away from him, will you? Don't never speak to him. If he comes in here you move clear to the other side of the room. Will you remember that, Lennie?

LENNIE

mourning: I don't want no trouble. I never done nothing to him!

GEORGE:

Well, that won't do you no good, if Curley wants to set himself up for a fighter. Just don't have nothing to do with him. Will you remember?

LENNIE:

Sure, George . . . I ain't gonna say a word. *Sounds of the teams coming in from the fields, jingling of harness, croak of heavy laden axles, men talking to and cussing the horses. Crack of a whip and from a distance a voice calling.*

SLIM'S VOICE:

Stable buck! Hey! Stable buck!

GEORGE:

Here come the guys. Just don't say nothing.

LENNIE

timidly: You ain't mad, George?

GEORGE:

I ain't mad at you. I'm mad at this here Curley bastard! I wanted we should get a little stake together. Maybe a hundred dollars. You keep away from Curley.

LENNIE:

Sure I will. I won't say a word.

GEORGE

hesitating: Don't let 'im pull you in—but—if the son-of-a-bitch socks you—let him have it!

LENNIE:

Let him have what, George?

GEORGE:

Never mind. . . . Look, if you get in any kind of trouble, you remember what I told you to do.

LENNIE:

If I get in any trouble, you ain't gonna let me tend the rabbits?

GEORGE:

That's not what I mean. You remember where we slept last night. Down by the river?

LENNIE:

Oh, sure I remember. I go there and hide in the brush until you come for me.

GEORGE:

That's it. Hide till I come for you. Don't let nobody see you. Hide in the brush by the river. Now say that over.

LENNIE:

Hide in the brush by the river. Down in the brush by the river.

GEORGE:

If you get in trouble.

LENNIE:

If I get in trouble.

A brake screeches outside and a call: "Stable buck, oh, stable buck!" "Where the hell's that goddamn nigger?" Suddenly Curley's Wife is standing in the door. Full, heavily rouged lips. Wide-spaced, made-up eyes, her fingernails are bright red, her hair hangs in little rolled clusters like sausages. She wears a cotton house dress and red mules, on the insteps of which are little bouquets of red ostrich feathers. George and Lennie look up at her.

Of Mice and Men

CURLEY'S WIFE:

I'm lookin' for Curley!

GEORGE

looks away from her: He was in here a minute ago but he went along.

CURLEY'S WIFE

puts her hands behind her back and leans against the door frame so that her body is thrown forward: You're the new fellas that just come, ain't you?

GEORGE

sullenly: Yeah.

CURLEY'S WIFE

bridles a little and inspects her fingernails: Sometimes Curley's in here.

GEORGE

brusquely: Well, he ain't now!

CURLEY'S WIFE

playfully: Well, if he ain't, I guess I'd better look some place else. *Lennie watches her, fascinated.*

GEORGE:

If I see Curley I'll pass the word you was lookin' for him.

CURLEY'S WIFE:

Nobody can't blame a person for lookin'.

60

GEORGE:

That depends what she's lookin' for.

CURLEY'S WIFE

a little wearily, dropping her coquetry: I'm jus' lookin' for somebody to talk to. Don't you never jus' want to talk to somebody?

SLIM

offstage: Okay! Put that lead pair in the north stalls.

CURLEY'S WIFE

to Slim, offstage: Hi, Slim!

SLIM

voice offstage: Hello.

CURLEY'S WIFE:

I—I'm tryin' to find Curley.

SLIM'S VOICE

offstage: Well, you ain't tryin' very hard. I seen him goin' in your house.

CURLEY'S WIFE

turning back toward George and Lennie: I gotta be goin'! *She exits hurriedly.*

GEORGE

looking around at Lennie: Jesus, what a tramp! So, that's what Curley picks for a wife. God Almighty, did you smell that stink she's got on? I can still smell her. Don't have to see *her* to know she's around.

LENNIE:

She's purty!

GEORGE:

Yeah. And she's sure hidin' it. Curley got his work ahead of him.

LENNIE

still staring at the doorway where she was: Gosh, she's purty!

GEORGE

turning furiously at him: Listen to me, you crazy bastard. Don't you even look at that bitch. I don't care what she says or what she does. I seen 'em poison before, but I ain't never seen no piece of jail bait worse than her. Don't you even smell near her!

LENNIE:

I never smelled, George!

GEORGE:

No, you never. But when she was standin' there showin' her legs, you wasn't lookin' the other way neither!

LENNIE:

I never meant no bad things, George. Honest I never.

GEORGE:

Well, you keep away from her. You let Curley take

the rap. He let himself in for it. *Disgustedly:* Glove full of vaseline. I bet he's eatin' raw eggs and writin' to patent-medicine houses.

LENNIE

cries out: I don't like this place. This ain't no good place. I don't like this place!

GEORGE:

Listen—I don't like it here no better than you do. But we gotta keep it till we get a stake. We're flat. We gotta get a stake. *Goes back to the table, thoughtfully:* If we can get just a few dollars in the poke we'll shove off and go up to the American River and pan gold. Guy can make a couple dollars a day there.

LENNIE

eagerly: Let's go, George. Let's get out of here. It's mean here.

GEORGE

shortly: I tell you we gotta stay a little while. We gotta get a stake. *The sounds of running water and rattle of basins are heard.* Shut up now, the guys'll be comin' in! *Pensively:* Maybe we ought to wash up. . . . But hell, we ain't done nothin' to get dirty.

SLIM

enters. He is a tall, dark man in blue jeans and a short denim jacket. He carries a crushed Stetson hat under

63

his arm and combs his long dark damp hair straight back. He stands and moves with a kind of majesty. He finishes combing his hair. Smoothes out his crushed hat, creases it in the middle and puts it on. In a gentle voice: It's brighter'n a bitch outside. Can't hardly see nothing in here. You the new guys?

GEORGE:

Just come.

SLIM:

Goin' to buck barley?

GEORGE:

That's what the boss says.

SLIM:

Hope you get on my team.

GEORGE:

Boss said we'd go with a jerk-line skinner named Slim.

SLIM:

That's me.

GEORGE:

You a jerk-line skinner?

SLIM

in self-disparagement: I can snap 'em around a little.

GEORGE

terribly impressed: That kinda makes you Jesus Christ on this ranch, don't it?

64

SLIM

obviously pleased: Oh, nuts!

GEORGE

chuckles: Like the man says, "The boss tells you what to do. But if you want to know how to do it, you got to ask the mule skinner." The man says any guy that can drive twelve Arizona jack rabbits with a jerk line can fall in a toilet and come up with a mince pie under each arm.

SLIM

laughing: Well, I hope you get on my team. I got a pair a punks that don't know a barley bag from a blue ball. You guys ever bucked any barley?

GEORGE:

Hell, yes. I ain't nothin' to scream about, but that big guy there can put up more grain alone than most pairs can.

SLIM

looks approvingly at George: You guys travel around together?

GEORGE:

Sure. We kinda look after each other. *Points at Lennie with his thumb:* He ain't bright. Hell of a good worker, though. Hell of a nice fella too. I've knowed him for a long time.

SLIM:

Ain't many guys travel around together. I don't know why. Maybe everybody in the whole damn world is scared of each other.

GEORGE:

It's a lot nicer to go 'round with a guy you know. You get used to it an' then it ain't no fun alone any more. *Enter Carlson. Big-stomached, powerful man. His head still drips water from scrubbing and dousing.*

CARLSON:

Hello, Slim! *He looks at George and Lennie.*

SLIM:

These guys just come.

CARLSON:

Glad to meet ya! My name's Carlson.

GEORGE:

I'm George Milton. This here's Lennie Small.

CARLSON:

Glad to meet you. He ain't very small. *Chuckles at his own joke:* He ain't small at all. Meant to ask you, Slim, how's your bitch? I seen she wasn't under your wagon this morning.

SLIM:

She slang her pups last night. Nine of 'em. I drownded four of 'em right off. She couldn't feed that many.

CARLSON:

Got five left, huh?

SLIM:

Yeah. Five. I kep' the biggest.

CARLSON:

What kinda dogs you think they gonna be?

SLIM:

I don't know. Some kind of shepherd, I guess. That's the most kind I seen around here when she's in heat.

CARLSON

laughs: I had an airedale an' a guy down the road got one of them little white floozy dogs, well, she was in heat and the guy locks her up. But my airedale, named Tom he was, he et a woodshed clear down to the roots to get to her. Guy come over one day, he's sore as hell, he says, "I wouldn't mind if my bitch had pups, but Christ Almighty, this morning she slang a litter of Shetland ponies. . . ." *Takes off his hat and scratches his head.* Got five pups, huh! Gonna keep all of 'em?

SLIM:

I don' know, gotta keep 'em awhile, so they can drink Lulu's milk.

CARLSON

thoughtfully: Well, looka here, Slim, I been thinkin'. That dog of Candy's is so goddamn old he can't hardly walk. Stinks like hell. Every time Candy brings him in the bunkhouse, I can smell him two or three days. Why don't you get Candy to shoot his ol' dog, and give him one of them pups to raise up? I can smell that dog a mile off. Got no teeth. Can't eat. Candy feeds him milk. He can't chew nothing else. And leadin' him around on a string so he don't bump into things . . . *The triangle outside begins to ring wildly. Continues for a few moments, then stops suddenly.* There she goes! *Outside there is a burst of voices as a group of men go by.*

SLIM

to Lennie and George: You guys better come on while they's still somethin' to eat. Won't be nothing left in a couple of minutes. *Exit Slim and Carlson, Lennie watches George excitedly.*

LENNIE:

George!

GEORGE

rumpling his cards into a pile: Yeah, I heard 'im, Lennie . . . I'll ask 'im!

LENNIE

excitedly: A brown and white one.

GEORGE:

Come on, let's get dinner. I don't know whether he's got a brown and white one.

LENNIE:

You ask him right away, George, so he won't kill no more of 'em!

GEORGE:

Sure! Come on now—le's go. *They start for the door.*

CURLEY

bounces in, angrily: You seen a girl around here?

GEORGE

coldly: 'Bout half an hour ago, mebbe.

CURLEY:

Well, what the hell was she doin'?

GEORGE

insultingly: She *said* she was lookin' for you.

CURLEY

measures both men with his eyes for a moment: Which way did she go?

GEORGE:

I don't know. I didn't watch her go. *Curley scowls at him a moment and then turns and hurries out the door.* You know, Lennie, I'm scared I'm gonna tangle with that bastard myself. I hate his guts! Jesus Christ, come on! They won't be a damn thing left to eat.

LENNIE:

Will you ask him about a brown and white one? *They exeunt.*

CURTAIN

ACT TWO

ACT TWO: SCENE I

About seven-thirty Friday evening.

Same bunkhouse interior as in last scene.

The evening light is seen coming in through the window, but it is quite dark in the interior of the bunkhouse.

From outside comes the sound of a horseshoe game. Thuds on the dirt and occasional clangs as a shoe hits the peg. Now and then voices are raised in approval or derision: "That's a good one." . . . "Goddamn right it's a good one." . . . "Here goes for a ringer. I need a ringer." . . . "Goddamn near got it, too."

Slim and George come into the darkening bunkhouse together. Slim reaches up and turns on the tin-shaded electric light. Sits down on a box at the table. George takes his place opposite.

SLIM:

It wasn't nothing. I would of had to drown most of them pups anyway. No need to thank me about that.

73

Of Mice and Men

GEORGE:

Wasn't much to you, mebbe, but it was a hell of a lot to him. Jesus Christ, I don't know how we're gonna get him to sleep in here. He'll want to stay right out in the barn. We gonna have trouble keepin' him from gettin' right in the box with them pups.

SLIM:

Say, you sure was right about him. Maybe he ain't bright—but I never seen such a worker. He damn near killed his partner buckin' barley. He'd take his end of that sack—*a gesture*—pretty near kill his partner. God Almighty, I never seen such a strong guy.

GEORGE

proudly: You just tell Lennie what to do and he'll do it if it don't take no figuring.

Outside the sound of the horseshoe game goes on: "Son of a bitch if I can win a goddamn game." . . . "Me neither. You'd think them shoes was anvils."

SLIM:

Funny how you and him string along together.

GEORGE:

What's so funny about it?

SLIM:

Oh, I don't know. Hardly none of the guys ever

travels around together. I hardly never seen two guys travel together. You know how the hands are. They come in and get their bunk and work a month and then they quit and go on alone. Never seem to give a damn about nobody. Jest seems kinda funny. A cuckoo like him and a smart guy like you traveling together.

GEORGE:

I ain't so bright neither or I wouldn't be buckin' barley for my fifty and found. If I was bright, if I was even a little bit smart, I'd have my own place and I'd be bringin' in my own crops 'stead of doin' all the work and not gettin' what comes up out of the ground. *He falls silent for a moment.*

SLIM:

A guy'd like to do that. Sometime I'd like to cuss a string of mules that was my own mules.

GEORGE:

It ain't so funny, him and me goin' round together. Him and me was both born in Auburn. I knowed his aunt. She took him when he was a baby and raised him up. When his aunt died Lennie jus' come along with me, out workin'. Got kinda used to each other after a little while.

75

SLIM:

Uh huh.

GEORGE:

First I used to have a hell of a lot of fun with him. Used to play jokes on him because he was too dumb to take care of himself. But, hell, he was too dumb even to know when he had a joke played on him. *Sarcastically:* Hell, yes, I had fun! Made me seem goddamn smart alongside of him.

SLIM:

I seen it that way.

GEORGE:

Why, he'd do any damn thing I tole him. If I tole him to walk over a cliff, over he'd go. You know that wasn't so damn much fun after a while. He never got mad about it, neither. I've beat hell out of him and he could bust every bone in my body jest with his hands. But he never lifted a finger against me.

SLIM

braiding a bull whip: Even if you socked him, wouldn't he?

GEORGE:

No, by God! I tell you what made me stop playing jokes. One day a bunch of guys was standin' aroun'

76

up on the Sacramento river. I was feelin' pretty smart. I turns to Lennie and I says, "Jump in."

SLIM:

What happened?

GEORGE:

He jumps. Couldn't swim a stroke. He damn near drowned. And he was so nice to me for pullin' him out. Clean forgot I tole him to jump in. Well, I ain't done nothin' like that no more. Makes me kinda sick tellin' about it.

SLIM:

He's a nice fella. A guy don't need no sense to be a nice fella. Seems to be sometimes it's jest the other way round. Take a real smart guy, he ain't hardly ever a nice fella.

GEORGE

stacking the scattered cards and getting his solitaire game ready again: I ain't got no people. I seen guys that go round on the ranches alone. That ain't no good. They don't have no fun. After a while they get mean.

SLIM

quietly: Yeah, I seen 'em get mean. I seen 'em get so they don't want to talk to nobody. Some ways they

77

got to. You take a bunch of guys all livin' in one room an' by God they got to mind their own business. 'Bout the only private thing a guy's got is where he come from and where he's goin'.

GEORGE:

'Course Lennie's a goddamn nuisance most of the time. But you get used to goin' round with a guy and you can't get rid of him. I mean you get used to him an' you can't get rid of bein' used to him. I'm sure drippin' at the mouth. I ain't told nobody all this before.

SLIM:

Do you want to git rid of him?

GEORGE:

Well, he gets in trouble all the time. Because he's so goddamn dumb. Like what happened in Weed. *He stops, alarmed at what he has said.* You wouldn't tell nobody?

SLIM

calmly: What did he do in Weed?

GEORGE:

You wouldn't tell?—No, course you wouldn't.

SLIM:

What did he do?

78

GEORGE:

Well, he seen this girl in a red dress. Dumb bastard like he is he wants to touch everything he likes. Jest wants to feel of it. So he reaches out to feel this red dress. Girl lets out a squawk and that gets Lennie all mixed up. He holds on 'cause that's the only thing he can think to do.

SLIM:

The hell!

GEORGE:

Well, this girl squawks her head off. I'm right close and I hear all the yellin', so I comes a-running. By that time Lennie's scared to death. You know, I had to sock him over the head with a fence picket to make him let go.

SLIM:

So what happens then?

GEORGE

carefully building his solitaire hand: Well, she runs in and tells the law she's been raped. The guys in Weed start out to lynch Lennie. So there we sit in an irrigation ditch, under water all the rest of that day. Got only our heads sticking out of water, up under the grass that grows out of the side of the ditch. That night we run outa there.

SLIM:

Didn't hurt the girl none, huh?

GEORGE:

Hell no, he jes' scared her.

SLIM:

He's a funny guy.

GEORGE:

Funny! Why, one time, you know what that big baby done! He was walking along a road—*Enter Lennie through the door. He wears his coat over his shoulder like a cape and walks hunched over.* Hi, Lennie. How do you like your pup?

LENNIE

breathlessly: He's brown and white jus' like I wanted. *Goes directly to his bunk and lies down. Face to the wall and knees drawn up.*

GEORGE

puts down his cards deliberately: Lennie!

LENNIE

over his shoulder: Huh? What you want George?

GEORGE

sternly: I tole ya, ya couldn't bring that pup in here.

LENNIE:

What pup, George? I ain't got no pup.

George goes quickly over to him, grabs him by the

shoulder and rolls him over. He picks up a tiny puppy from where Lennie has been concealing it against his stomach.

LENNIE

quickly: Give him to me, George.

GEORGE:

You get right up and take this pup to the nest. He's got to sleep with his mother. Ya want ta kill him? Jes' born last night and ya take him out of the nest. Ya take him back or I'll tell Slim not to let you have him.

LENNIE

pleadingly: Give him to me, George. I'll take him back. I didn't mean no bad thing, George. Honest I didn't. I jus' want to pet him a little.

GEORGE

giving the pup to him: All right, you get him back there quick. And don't you take him out no more.

LENNIE

scuttles out of the room.

SLIM:

Jesus, he's just like a kid, ain't he?

GEORGE:

Sure he's like a kid. There ain't no more harm in him

81

than a kid neither, except he's so strong. I bet he won't come in here to sleep tonight. He'll sleep right alongside that box in the barn. Well, let him. He ain't doin' no harm out there. *The light has faded out outside and it appears quite dark outside. Enter Candy leading his old dog by a string.*

CANDY:

Hello, Slim. Hello, George. Didn't neither of you play horseshoes?

SLIM:

I don't like to play every night.

CANDY

goes to his bunk and sits down, presses the old blind dog to the floor beside him: Either you guys got a slug of whiskey? I got a gut ache.

SLIM:

I ain't. I'd drink it myself if I had. And I ain't got no gut ache either.

CANDY:

Goddamn cabbage give it to me. I knowed it was goin' to before I ever et it. *Enter Carlson and Whit.*

CARLSON:

Jesus, how that nigger can pitch shoes!

SLIM:

He's plenty good.

WHIT:

Damn right he is.

CARLSON:

Yeah. He don't give nobody else a chance to win. *Stops and sniffs the air. Looks around until he sees Candy's dog:* God Almighty, that dog stinks. Get him outa here, Candy. I don't know nothing that stinks as bad as ole dogs. You got to get him outa here.

CANDY

lying down on his bunk, reaches over and pats the ancient dog, speaks softly: I been round him so much I never notice how he stinks.

CARLSON:

Well, I can't stand him in here. That stink hangs round even after he's gone. *Walks over and stands looking down at the dog:* Got no teeth. All stiff with rheumatism. He ain't no good to you, Candy. Why don't you shoot him?

CANDY

uncomfortably: Well, hell, I had him so long! Had him since he was a pup. I herded sheep with him. *Proudly:*

You wouldn't think it to look at him now. He was the best damn sheep dog I ever seen.

GEORGE:

I knowed a guy in Weed that had an airedale that could herd sheep. Learned it from the other dogs.

CARLSON

sticking to his point: Lookit, Candy. This ole dog jus' suffers itself all the time. If you was to take him out and shoot him—right in the back of the head . . . *Leans over and points:* . . . right there, why he never'd know what hit him.

CANDY

unhappily: No, I couldn't do that. I had him too long.

CARLSON

insisting: He don't have no fun no more. He stinks like hell. Tell you what I'll do. I'll shoot him for you. Then it won't be you that done it.

CANDY

sits up on the bunk, rubbing his whiskers nervously, speaks plaintively: I had him from a pup.

WHIT:

Let 'im alone, Carl. It ain't a guy's dog that matters. It's the way the guy feels about the dog. Hell, I had a mutt once I wouldn't a traded for a field trial pointer.

CARLSON

being persuasive: Well, Candy ain't being nice to him, keeping him alive. Lookit, Slim's bitch got a litter right now. I bet you Slim would give ya one of them pups to raise up, wouldn't ya, Slim?

SLIM

studying the dog: Yeah. You can have a pup if you want to.

CANDY

helplessly: Mebbe it would hurt. *After a moment's pause, positively:* And I don't mind taking care of him.

CARLSON:

Aw, he'd be better off dead. The way I'd shoot him he wouldn't feel nothin'. I'd put the gun right there. *Points with his toe:* Right back of the head.

WHIT:

Aw, let 'im alone, Carl.

CARLSON:

Why, hell, he wouldn't even quiver.

WHIT:

Let 'im alone. *He produces a magazine.* Say, did you see this? Did you see this in the book here?

CARLSON:

See what?

85

WHIT:

Right there. Read that.

CARLSON:

I don't want to read nothing. . . . It'd be all over in a minute, Candy. Come on.

WHIT:

Did you see it, Slim? Go on, read it. Read it out loud.

SLIM:

What is it?

WHIT:

Read it.

SLIM

reads slowly: "Dear Editor: I read your mag for six years and I think it is the best on the market. I like stories by Peter Rand. I think he is a whing-ding. Give us more like the Dark Rider. I don't write many letters. Just thought I would tell you I think your mag is the best dime's worth I ever spen'." *Looks up questioningly.* What you want me to read that for?

WHIT:

Go on, read the name at the bottom.

SLIM

reading: "Yours for Success, William Tenner." *Looks up at Whit.* What ya want me to read that for?

CARLSON:

Come on, Candy—what you say?

WHIT

*taking the magazine and closing it impressively. Talks
to cover Carlson:* You don't remember Bill Tenner?
Worked here about three months ago?

SLIM

thinking: Little guy? Drove a cultivator?

WHIT:

That's him. That's the guy.

CARLSON

has refused to be drawn into this conversation: Look,
Candy. If you want me to, I'll put the old devil outa
his misery right now and get it over with. There ain't
nothin' left for him. Can't eat, can't see, can't hardly
walk. Tomorrow you can pick one of Slim's pups.

SLIM:

Sure . . . I got a lot of 'em.

CANDY

hopefully: You ain't got no gun.

CARLSON:

The hell, I ain't. Got a Luger. It won't hurt him
none at all.

CANDY:

Mebbe tomorrow. Let's wait till tomorrow.

87

CARLSON:

I don't see no reason for it. *Goes to his bunk, pulls a bag from underneath, takes a Luger pistol out.* Let's get it over with. We can't sleep with him stinking around in here. *He snaps a shell into the chamber, sets the safety and puts the pistol into his hip pocket.*

SLIM

as Candy looks toward him for help: Better let him go, Candy.

CANDY

looks at each person for some hope. Whit makes a gesture of protest and then resigns himself. The others look away, to avoid responsibility. At last, very softly and hopelessly: All right. Take him.

He doesn't look down at the dog at all. Lies back on his bunk and crosses his arms behind his head and stares at the ceiling. Carlson picks up the string, helps the dog to its feet.

CARLSON:

Come, boy. Come on, boy. *To Candy, apologetically:* He won't even feel it. *Candy does not move nor answer him.* Come on, boy. That's the stuff. Come on. *He leads the dog toward the door.*

SLIM:

Carlson?

CARLSON:

Yeah.

SLIM

curtly: Take a shovel.

CARLSON:

Oh, sure, I get you.

Exit Carlson with the dog. George follows to the door, shuts it carefully and sets the latch. Candy lies rigidly on his bunk. The next scene is one of silence and quick staccato speeches.

SLIM

loudly: One of my lead mules got a bad hoof. Got to get some tar on it. *There is a silence.*

GEORGE

loudly: Anybody like to play a little euchre?

WHIT:

I'll lay out a few with you.

They take places opposite each other at the table but George does not shuffle the cards. He ripples the edge of the deck. Everybody looks over at him. He stops. Silence again.

SLIM

compassionately: Candy, you can have any of them pups you want. *There is no answer from Candy. There is a little gnawing noise on the stage.*

GEORGE:

Sounds like there was a rat under there. We ought to set a trap there. *Deep silence again.*

WHIT

exasperated: What the hell is takin' him so long? Lay out some cards, why don't you? We ain't gonna get no euchre played this way.

George studies the backs of the cards. And after a long silence there is a shot in the distance. All the men start a bit, look quickly at Candy. For a moment he continues to stare at the ceiling and then rolls slowly over and faces the wall. George shuffles the cards noisily and deals them.

GEORGE:

Well, let's get to it.

WHIT

still to cover the moment: Yeah . . . I guess you guys really come here to work, huh?

GEORGE:

How do you mean?

WHIT

chuckles: Well, you come on a Friday. You got two days to work till Sunday.

GEORGE:

I don't see how you figure.

90

WHIT:

You do if you been round these big ranches much. A guy that wants to look over a ranch comes in Saturday afternoon. He gets Saturday night supper, three meals on Sunday and he can quit Monday morning after breakfast without turning a hand. But you come to work on Friday noon. You got ta put in a day and a half no matter how ya figure it.

GEORGE

quietly: We're goin' stick around awhile. Me and Lennie's gonna roll up a stake. *Door opens and the Negro stable buck puts in his head. A lean-faced Negro with pained eyes.*

CROOKS:

Mr. Slim.

SLIM

who has been watching Candy the whole time: Huh? Oh, hello, Crooks, what's the matter?

CROOKS:

You tole me to warm up tar for that mule's foot. I got it warm now.

SLIM:

Oh, sure, Crooks. I'll come right out and put it on.

CROOKS:

I can do it for you if you want, Mr. Slim.

SLIM

standing up: Naw, I'll take care of my own team.

CROOKS:

Mr. Slim.

SLIM:

Yeah.

CROOKS:

That big new guy is messing round your pups in the barn.

SLIM:

Well, he ain't doin' no harm. I give him one of them pups.

CROOKS:

Just thought I'd tell ya. He's takin' 'em out of the nest and handling 'em. That won't do 'em no good.

SLIM:

Oh, he won't hurt 'em.

GEORGE

looks up from his cards: If that crazy bastard is foolin' round too much jus' kick him out. *Slim follows the stable buck out.*

WHIT

examining his cards: Seen the new kid yet?

GEORGE:

What kid?

WHIT:

Why, Curley's new wife.

GEORGE

cautiously: Yeah, I seen her.

WHIT:

Well, ain't she a lulu?

GEORGE:

I ain't seen that much of her.

WHIT:

Well, you stick around and keep your eyes open. You'll see plenty of her. I never seen nobody like her. She's just workin' on everybody all the time. Seems like she's even workin' on the stable buck. I don't know what the hell she wants.

GEORGE

casually: Been any trouble since she got here? *Obviously neither man is interested in the card game. Whit lays down his hand and George gathers the cards in and lays out a solitaire hand.*

WHIT:

I see what you mean. No, they ain't been no trouble

93

yet. She's only been here a couple of weeks. Curley's got yellow jackets in his drawers, but that's all so far. Every time the guys is around she shows up. She's lookin' for Curley. Or she thought she left somethin' layin' around and she's lookin' for that. Seems like she can't keep away from guys. And Curley's runnin' round like a cat lookin' for a dirt road. But they ain't been no trouble.

GEORGE:

Ranch with a bunch of guys on it ain't no place for a girl. Specially like her.

WHIT:

If she's give you any ideas you ought to come in town with us guys tomorrow night.

GEORGE:

Why, what's doin'?

WHIT:

Just the usual thing. We go in to old Susy's place. Hell of a nice place. Old Susy is a laugh. Always cracking jokes. Like she says when we come up on the front porch last Saturday night: Susy opens the door and she yells over her shoulder: "Get your coats on, girls, here comes the sheriff." She never talks dirty neither. Got five girls there.

GEORGE:

What does it set you back?

WHIT:

Two and a half. You can get a shot of whiskey for
fifteen cents. Susy got nice chairs to set in too. If a
guy don't want to flop, why, he can just set in them
chairs and have a couple or three shots and just pass
the time of day. Susy don't give a damn. She ain't
rushin' guys through, or kicking them out if they
don't want to flop.

GEORGE:

Might go in and look the joint over.

WHIT:

Sure. Come along. It's a hell of a lot of fun—her
crackin' jokes all the time. Like she says one time, she
says: "I've knew people that if they got a rag rug on
the floor and a kewpie doll lamp on the phonograph
they think they're runnin' a parlor house." That's
Gladys's house she's talkin' about. And Susy says: "I
know what you boys want," she says: "My girls is
clean," she says. "And there ain't no water in my
whiskey," she says. "If any you guys want to look
at a kewpie doll lamp and take your chance of gettin'
burned, why, you know where to go." She says:

"They's guys round here walkin' bowlegged because they liked to look at a kewpie doll lamp."

GEORGE:

Gladys runs the other house, huh?

WHIT:

Yeah. *Enter Carlson. Candy looks at him.*

CARLSON:

God, it's a dark night. *Goes to his bunk; starts cleaning his pistol.*

WHIT:

We don't never go to Gladys's. Gladys gits three bucks, and two bits a shot and she don't crack no jokes. But Susy's place is clean and she got nice chairs. A guy can set in there like he lived there. Don't let no Manila Goo-Goos in, neither.

GEORGE:

Aw, I don't know. Me and Lennie's rollin' up a stake. I might go in and set and have a shot, but I ain't puttin' out no two and a half.

WHIT:

Well, a guy got to have some fun sometimes. *Enter Lennie. Lennie creeps to his bunk and sits down.*

GEORGE:

Didn't bring him back in, did you, Lennie?

LENNIE:

No, George, honest I didn't. See?

WHIT:

Say, how about this euchre game?

GEORGE:

Okay. I didn't think you wanted to play. *Enter Curley excitedly.*

CURLEY:

Any you guys seen my wife?

WHIT:

She ain't been here.

CURLEY

looks theateningly about the room: Where the hell's Slim?

GEORGE:

Went out in the barn. He was goin' put some tar on a split hoof.

CURLEY:

How long ago did he go?

GEORGE:

Oh, five, ten miutes. *Curley jumps out the door.*

WHIT

standing up: I guess maybe I'd like to see this. Curley must be spoilin' or he wouldn't start for Slim. Curley's

97

handy, goddamn handy. But just the same he better leave Slim alone.

GEORGE:

Thinks Slim's with his wife, don't he?

WHIT:

Looks like it. 'Course Slim ain't. Least I don't think Slim is. But I like to see the fuss if it comes off. Come on, le's go.

GEORGE:

I don't want to git mixed up in nothing. Me and Lennie got to make a stake.

CARLSON

finishes cleaning gun, puts it in his bag and stands up: I'll look her over. Ain't seen a good fight in a hell of a while. *Whit and Carlson exeunt.*

GEORGE:

You see Slim out in the barn?

LENNIE:

Sure. He tole me I better not pet that pup no more, like I said.

GEORGE:

Did you see that girl out there?

LENNIE:

You mean Curley's girl?

GEORGE:

Yeah. Did she come in the barn?

LENNIE

cautiously: No—anyways I never seen her.

GEORGE:

You never seen Slim talkin' to her?

LENNIE:

Uh-uh. She ain't been in the barn.

GEORGE:

Okay. I guess them guys ain't gonna see no fight. If they's any fightin', Lennie, ya get out of the way and stay out.

LENNIE:

I don't want no fight. *George lays out his solitaire hand. Lennie picks up a face card and studies it. Turns it over and studies it again.* Both ends the same. George, why is it both ends the same?

GEORGE:

I don't know. That jus' the way they make 'em. What was Slim doin' in the barn when you seen him?

LENNIE:

Slim?

GEORGE:

Sure, you seen him in the barn. He tole you not to pet the pups so much.

LENNIE:

Oh. Yeah. He had a can of tar and a paint brush. I don't know what for.

GEORGE:

You sure that girl didn't come in like she come in here today?

LENNIE:

No, she never come.

GEORGE

sighs: You give me a good whorehouse every time. A guy can go in and get drunk and get it over all at once and no messes. And he knows how much it's goin' set him back. These tarts is jus' buckshot to a guy. *Lennie listens with admiration, moving his lips, and George continues.* You remember Andy Cushman, Lennie? Went to grammar school same time as us?

LENNIE:

The one that his ole lady used to make hot cakes for the kids?

GEORGE:

Yeah. That's the one. You can remember if they's somepin to eat in it. *Scores up some cards in his solitaire playing.* Well, Andy's in San Quentin right now on account of a tart.

LENNIE:

George?

GEORGE:

Huh?

LENNIE:

How long is it goin' be till we git that little place to live on the fat of the land?

GEORGE:

I don't know. We gotta get a big stake together. I know a little place we can get cheap, but they ain't givin' it away. *Candy turns slowly over and watches George.*

LENNIE:

Tell about that place, George.

GEORGE:

I jus' tole you. Jus' last night.

LENNIE:

Go on, tell again.

GEORGE:

Well, it's ten acres. Got a little windmill. Got a little shack on it and a chicken run. Got a kitchen orchard. Cherries, apples, peaches, 'cots and nuts. Got a few berries. There's a place for alfalfa and plenty water to flood it. There's a pig pen. . . .

LENNIE

breaking in: And rabbits, George?

GEORGE:

I could easy build a few hutches. And you could feed alfalfa to them rabbits.

LENNIE:

Damn right I could. *Excitedly:* You goddamn right I could.

GEORGE

his voice growing warmer: And we could have a few pigs. I'd build a smokehouse. And when we kill a pig we could smoke the hams. When the salmon run up the river we can catch a hundred of 'em. Every Sunday we'd kill a chicken or rabbit. Mebbe we'll have a cow or a goat. And the cream is so goddamn thick you got to cut it off the pan with a knife.

LENNIE

watching him with wide eyes, softly: We can live off the fat of the land.

GEORGE:

Sure. All kinds of vegetables in the garden and if we want a little whiskey we can sell some eggs or somethin'. And we wouldn't sleep in no bunkhouse. Nobody could can us in the middle of a job.

LENNIE

begging: Tell about the house, George.

GEORGE:

Sure. We'd have a little house. And a room to our-selves. And it ain't enough land so we'd have to work too hard. Mebbe six, seven hours a day only. We wouldn't have to buck no barley eleven hours a day. And when we put in a crop, why we'd be there to take that crop up. We'd know what come of our planting.

LENNIE

eagerly: And rabbits. And I'd take care of them. Tell how I'd do that, George.

GEORGE:

Sure. You'd go out in the alfalfa patch and you'd have a sack. You'd fill up the sack and bring it in and put it in the rabbit cages.

LENNIE:

They'd nibble and they'd nibble, the way they do. I seen 'em.

GEORGE:

Every six weeks or so them does would throw a litter. So we'd have plenty rabbits to eat or sell. *Pauses for inspiration.* And we'd keep a few pigeons to go flying round and round the windmill, like they done when I was a kid. *Seems entranced.* And it'd be our own. And nobody could can us. If we don't like a guy we can say: "Get to hell out," and by God he's got to do it. And if a friend come along, why, we'd have an extra bunk. Know what we'd say? We'd say, "Why don't you spen' the night?" And by God he would. We'd have a setter dog and a couple of striped cats. *Looks sharply at Lennie.* But you gotta watch out them cats don't get the little rabbits.

LENNIE

breathing hard: You jus' let 'em try. I'll break their goddamn necks. I'll smash them cats flat with a stick. I'd smash 'em flat with a stick. That's what I'd do. *They sit silently for a moment.*

CANDY

at the sound of his voice, both Lennie and George jump as though caught in some secret: You know where's a place like that?

GEORGE

solemnly: S'pose I do, what's that to you?

CANDY:

You don't need to tell me where it's at. Might be any place.

GEORGE

relieved: Sure. That's right, you couldn't find it in a hundred years.

CANDY

excitedly: How much they want for a place like that?

GEORGE

grudgingly: Well, I could get it for six hundred bucks. The ole people that owns it is flat bust. And the ole lady needs medicine. Say, what's it to you? You got nothing to do with us!

CANDY

softly: I ain't much good with only one hand. I lost my hand right here on the ranch. That's why they didn't can me. They give me a job swampin'. And they give me two hundred and fifty dollars 'cause I lost my hand. An' I got fifty more saved up right in the bank right now. That's three hundred. And I got forty more comin' the end of the month. Tell you what . . . *He leans forward eagerly.* S'pose I went in with you guys? That's three hundred and forty bucks I'd put in. I ain't much good, but I could cook and tend the chickens and hoe the garden some. How'd that be?

GEORGE

his eyes half closed, uncertainly: I got to think about

that. We was always goin' to do it by ourselves. Me an' Lennie. I never thought of nobody else.

CANDY:

I'd make a will. Leave my share to you guys in case I kicked off. I ain't got no relations nor nothing. You fellas got any money? Maybe we could go there right now.

GEORGE

disgustedly: We got ten bucks between us. *He thinks.* Say, look. If me and Lennie work a month and don't spend nothing at all, we'll have a hundred bucks. That would be four forty. I bet we could swing her for that. Then you and Lennie could go get her started and I'd get a job and make up the rest. You could sell eggs and stuff like that. *They look at each other in amazement. Reverently:* Jesus Christ, I bet we could swing her. *His voice is full of wonder:* I bet we could swing 'er.

CANDY

scratches the stump of his wrist nervously: I got hurt four years ago. They'll can me pretty soon. Jest as soon as I can't swamp out no bunkhouses they'll put me on the county. Maybe if I give you guys my

106

money, you'll let me hoe in the garden, even when I ain't no good at it. And I'll wash dishes and little chicken stuff like that. But hell, I'll be on our own place. I'll be let to work on our own place. *Miserably:* You seen what they done to my dog. They says he wasn't no good to himself nor nobody else. But when I'm that way nobody'll shoot me. I wish somebody would. They won't do nothing like that. I won't have no place to go and I can't get no more jobs.

GEORGE

stands up: We'll do 'er! God damn, we'll fix up that little ole place and we'll go live there. *Wonderingly:* S'pose they was a carnival, or a circus come to town or a ball game or any damn thing. *Candy nods in appreciation:* We'd just go to her. We wouldn't ask nobody if we could. Just say we'll go to her, by God, and we would. Just milk the cow and sling some grain to the chickens and go to her.

LENNIE:

And put some grass to the rabbits. I wouldn't forget to feed them. When we gonna to do it, George?

GEORGE

decisively: In one month. Right squack in one month.

107

Know what I'm gonna do? I'm goin' write to them ole people that owns the place that we'll take 'er. And Candy'll send a hundred dollars to bind her.

CANDY

happily: I sure will. They got a good stove there?

GEORGE:

Sure, got a nice stove. Burns coal or wood.

LENNIE:

I'm gonna take my pup. I bet by Christ he likes it there. *The window, center backstage, swings outward. Curley's Wife looks in. They do not see her.*

GEORGE

quickly: Now don't tell nobody about her. Jus' us three and nobody else. They'll liable to can us so we can't make no stake. We'll just go on like we was a bunch of punks. Like we was gonna buck barley the rest of our lives. And then all of a sudden, one day, bang! We get our pay and scram out of here.

CANDY:

I can give you three hundred right now.

LENNIE:

And not tell nobody. We won't tell nobody, George.

GEORGE:

You're goddamn right we won't. *There is a silence and*

then George speaks irritably. You know, seems to me I can almost smell that carnation stuff that goddamn tart dumps on herself.

CURLEY'S WIFE

in the first part of the speech by George she starts to step out of sight but at the last words her face darkens with anger. At her first words everybody in the room looks around at her and remains rigid during her tirade: Who you callin' a tart! I come from a nice home. I was brung up by nice people. Nobody never got to me before I was married. I was straight. I tell you I was good. *A little plaintively:* I was. *Angrily again:* You know Curley. You know he wouldn't stay with me if he wasn't sure. I tell you Curley is sure. You got no right to call me a tart.

GEORGE

sullenly: If you ain't a tart, what you always hangin' round guys for? You got a house an' you got a man. We don't want no trouble from you.

CURLEY'S WIFE

pleadingly: Sure I got a man. He ain't never home. I got nobody to talk to. I got nobody to be with. Think I can just sit home and do nothin' but cook for Curley? I want to see somebody. Just see 'em an' talk to 'em. There ain't no women. I can't walk to town. And Curley don't take me to no dances now. I tell you I jus' want to talk to somebody.

GEORGE

boldly: If you're just friendly what you givin' out the eye for an' floppin' your can around?

CURLEY'S WIFE

sadly: I just wanta be nice.

The sound of approaching voices: "You don't have to get mad about it, do you?" . . . "I ain't mad, but I just don't want no more questions, that's all. I just don't want no more questions."

GEORGE:

Get goin'. We don't want no trouble.

Curley's Wife looks from the window and closes it silently and disappears. Enter Slim, followed by Curley, Carlson and Whit. Slim's hands are black with tar. Curley hangs close to his elbow.

CURLEY

explaining: Well, I didn't mean nothing, Slim. I jus' ast you.

SLIM:

Well, you been askin' too often. I'm gettin' goddamn

sick of it. If you can't look after your own wife, what you expect me to do about it? You lay off of me.

CURLEY:

I'm jus' tryin' to tell you I didn't mean nothing. I just thought you might of saw her.

CARLSON:

Why don't you tell her to stay to hell home where she belongs? You let her hang around the bunkhouses and pretty soon you're goin' have somethin' on your hands.

CURLEY

whirls on Carlson: You keep out of this 'less you want ta step outside.

CARLSON

laughing: Why you goddamn punk. You tried to throw a scare into Slim and you couldn't make it stick. Slim throwed a scare into you. You're yellow as a frog's belly. I don't care if you're the best boxer in the country, you come for me and I'll kick your goddamn head off.

WHIT

joining in the attack: Glove full of vaseline!

CURLEY

glares at him, then suddenly sniffs the air, like a hound:

111

By God, she's been in *here*. I can smell— By God, she's
been in here. *To George:* You was here. The other
guys was outside. Now, God damn you—you talk.

CURLEY

GEORGE

*looks worried. He seems to make up his mind to face
an inevitable situation. Stands up. Slowly takes off his
coat, and folds it almost daintily. Speaks in an unemo-
tional monotone:* Somebody got to beat the hell outa
you. I guess I'm elected. *Lennie has been watching,
fascinated. He gives his high, nervous chuckle.*

CURLEY

whirls on him: What the hell you laughin' at?

LENNIE

blankly: Huh?

CURLEY

exploding with rage: Come on, you big bastard. Get up
on your feet. No big son-of-a-bitch is gonna laugh at
me. I'll show you who's yellow.

*Lennie looks helplessly at George. Gets up and tries
to retreat upstage. Curley follows slashing at him. The
others mass themselves in front of the two contestants:
"That ain't no way, Curley—he ain't done nothing to
you." . . . "Lay off him, will you, Curley. He ain't no*

fighter." ... "Sock him back, big guy! Don't be afraid of him!" ... "Give him a chance, Curley. Give him a chance."

LENNIE

crying with terror: George, make him leave me alone, George.

GEORGE:

Get him, Lennie. Get him! *There is a sharp cry. The gathering of men opens and Curley is flopping about, his hand lost in Lennie's hand.* Let go of him, Lennie. Let go! *"He's got his hand!"* ... *"Look at that, will you?"* ... *"Jesus, what a guy!" Lennie watches in terror the flopping man he holds. Lennie's face is covered with blood. George slaps Lennie in the face again and again. Curley is weak and shrunken.* Let go his hand, Lennie. Slim, come help me, while this guy's got any hand left. *Suddenly Lennie lets go. He cowers away from George.*

LENNIE:

You told me to, George. I heard you tell me to. *Curley has dropped to the floor. Slim and Carlson bend over him and look at his hand. Slim looks over at Lennie with horror.*

SLIM:

We got to get him to a doctor. It looks to me like every bone in his hand is busted.

LENNIE

crying: I didn't wanta. I didn't wanta hurt 'im.

SLIM:

Carlson, you get the candy wagon out. He'll have to go into Soledad and get his hand fixed up. *Turns to the whimpering Lennie:* It ain't your fault. This punk had it comin' to him. But Jesus—he ain't hardly got no hand left.

GEORGE

moving near: Slim, will we git canned now? Will Curley's ole man can us now?

SLIM:

I don't know. *Kneels down beside Curley:* You got your sense enough to listen? *Curley nods:* Well, then you listen. I think you got your hand caught in a machine. If you don't tell nobody what happened, we won't. But you jest tell and try to get this guy canned and we'll tell everybody. And then will you get the laugh! *Helps Curley to his feet.* Come on now. Carlson's goin' to take you in to a doctor. *Starts for*

114

the door, turns back to Lennie: Le's see your hands.
Lennie sticks out both hands: Christ Almighty!

GEORGE:

Lennie was just scairt. He didn't know what to do.
I tole you nobody ought never to fight him. No, I
guess it was Candy I tole.

CANDY

solemnly: That's just what you done. Right this morning when Curley first lit into him. You says he better
not fool with Lennie if he knows what's good for
him. *They all leave the stage except George and Lennie
and Candy.*

GEORGE

to Lennie, very gently: It ain't your fault. You don't
need to be scairt no more. You done jus' what I tole
you to. Maybe you better go in the washroom and
clean up your face. You look like hell.

LENNIE:

I didn't want no trouble.

GEORGE:

Come on—I'll go with you.

LENNIE:

George?

Of Mice and Men

GEORGE:

What you want?

LENNIE:

Can I still tend the rabbits, George?

*They exeunt together, side by side, through the door
of the bunkhouse.*

CURTAIN

ACT TWO: SCENE II

Ten o'clock Saturday evening.

The room of the stable buck, a lean-to off the barn. There is a plank door up stage center; a small square window center right. On one side of the door a leather working bench with tools racked behind it, and on the other racks with broken and partly mended harnesses, collars, hames, traces, etc. At the left upstage Crooks' bunk. Over it two shelves. On one a great number of medicines in cans and bottles. And on the other a number of tattered books and a big alarm clock. In the corner right upstage a single-barreled shotgun and on the floor beside it a pair of rubber boots. A large pair of gold spectacles hangs on a nail over Crooks' bunk.

The entrance leads into the barn proper. From that direction and during the whole scene come the sounds of horses eating, stamping, jingling their halter chains and now and then whinnying.

Two empty nail kegs are in the room to be used as

seats. *Single unshaded small-candle-power carbon light hanging from its own cord.*

As the curtain rises, we see Crooks sitting on his bunk rubbing his back with liniment. He reaches up under his shirt to do this. His face is lined with pain. As he rubs he flexes his muscles and shivers a little.

Lennie appears in the open doorway, nearly filling the opening. Then Crooks, sensing his presence, raises his eyes, stiffens and scowls.

Lennie smiles in an attempt to make friends.

CROOKS

sharply: You got no right to come in my room. This here's my room. Nobody got any right in here but me.

LENNIE

fawning: I ain't doin' nothing. Just come in the barn to look at my pup, and I seen your light.

CROOKS:

Well, I got a right to have a light. You go on and get out of my room. I ain't wanted in the bunkhouse and you ain't wanted in my room.

LENNIE

ingenuously: Why ain't you wanted?

CROOKS

furiously: 'Cause I'm black. They play cards in there.

But I can't play because I'm black. They say I stink. Well, I tell you all of you stink to me.

LENNIE

helplessly: Everybody went into town. Slim and George and everybody. George says I got to stay here and not get into no trouble. I seen your light.

CROOKS:

Well, what do you want?

LENNIE:

Nothing . . . I seen your light. I thought I could jus' come in and set.

CROOKS

stares at Lennie for a moment, takes down his spectacles and adjusts them over his ears; says in a complaining tone: I don't know what you're doin' in the barn anyway. You ain't no skinner. There's no call for a bucker to come into the barn at all. You've got nothing to do with the horses and mules.

LENNIE

patiently: The pup. I come to see my pup.

CROOKS:

Well, God damn it, go and see your pup then. Don't go no place where you ain't wanted.

Of Mice and Men

LENNIE

> *advances a step into the room, remembers and backs to the door again:* I looked at him a little. Slim says I ain't to pet him very much.

CROOKS

> *the anger gradually going out of his voice:* Well, you been taking him out of the nest all the time. I wonder the ole lady don't move him some place else.

LENNIE

> *moving into the room:* Oh, she don't care. She lets me.

CROOKS

> *scowls and then gives up:* Come on in and set awhile. Long as you won't get out and leave me alone, you might as well set down. *A little more friendly:* All the boys gone into town, huh?

LENNIE:

> All but old Candy. He jus' sets in the bunkhouse sharpening his pencils. And sharpening and figurin'.

CROOKS

> *adjusting his glasses:* Figurin'? What's Candy figurin' about?

LENNIE:

> 'Bout the land. 'Bout the little place.

CROOKS:

You're nuts. You're crazy as a wedge. What land you talkin' about?

LENNIE:

The land we're goin' ta get. And a little house and pigeons.

CROOKS:

Just nuts. I don't blame the guy you're traveling with for keeping you out of sight.

LENNIE

quietly: It ain't no lie. We're gonna do it. Gonna get a little place and live on the fat of the land.

CROOKS

settling himself comfortably on his bunk: Set down. Set down on that nail keg.

LENNIE

hunches over on the little barrel: You think it's a lie. But it ain't no lie. Ever' word's the truth. You can ask George.

CROOKS

puts his dark chin on his palm: You travel round with George, don't you?

LENNIE

proudly: Sure, me and him goes ever' place together.

CROOKS

after a pause, quietly: Sometimes he talks and you don't know what the hell he's talkin' about. Ain't that so? *Leans forward.* Ain't that so?

LENNIE:

Yeah. Sometimes.

CROOKS:

Just talks on. And you don't know what the hell it's all about.

LENNIE:

How long you think it'll be before them pups will be old enough to pet?

CROOKS

laughs again: A guy can talk to you and be sure you won't go blabbin'. A couple of weeks and them pups will be all right. *Musing:* George knows what he's about. Just talks and you don't understand nothing. *Mood gradually changes to excitement:* Well, this is just a nigger talkin' and a busted-back nigger. It don't mean nothing, see. You couldn't remember it anyway. I seen it over and over—a guy talking to another guy and it don't make no difference if he don't hear or understand. The thing is they're talkin'. *He pounds*

122

his knee with his hand. George can tell you screwy things and it don't matter. It's just the talkin'. It's just bein' with another guy, that's all. *His voice becomes soft and malicious:* S'pose George don't come back no more? S'pose he took a powder and just ain't comin' back. What you do then?

LENNIE

trying to follow Crooks: What? What?

CROOKS:

I said s'pose George went into town tonight and you never heard of him no more. *Presses forward:* Just s'pose that.

LENNIE

sharply: He won't do it. George wouldn't do nothing like that. I been with George a long time. He'll come back tonight. . . . *Doubt creeps into his voice:* Don't you think he will?

CROOKS

delighted with his torture: Nobody can tell what a guy will do. Let's say he wants to come back and can't. S'pose he gets killed or hurt so he can't come back.

LENNIE

in terrible apprehension: I don't know. Say, what you doin' anyway? It ain't true. George ain't got hurt.

CROOKS

cruelly: Want me to tell you what'll happen? They'll take you to the booby hatch. They'll tie you up with a collar like a dog. Then you'll be jus' like me. Livin' in a kennel.

LENNIE

furious, walks over towards Crooks: Who hurt George?

CROOKS

recoiling from him with fright: I was just supposin'. George ain't hurt. He's all right. He'll be back all right.

LENNIE

standing over him: What you supposin' for? Ain't nobody goin' to s'pose any hurt to George.

CROOKS

trying to calm him: Now set down. George ain't hurt. Go on now, set down.

LENNIE

growling: Ain't nobody gonna talk no hurt to George.

CROOKS

very gently: Maybe you can see now. You got George. You know he's comin' back. S'pose you didn't have nobody. S'pose you couldn't go in the bunkhouse and play rummy, 'cause you was black. How would you

124

like that? S'pose you had to set out here and read books. Sure, you could play horseshoes until it got dark, but then you got to read books. Books ain't no good. A guy needs somebody . . . to be near him. *His tone whines:* A guy goes nuts if he ain't got nobody. Don't make no difference who it is as long as he's with you. I tell you a guy gets too lonely, he gets sick.

CROOKS

reassuring himself: George gonna come back. Maybe George come back already. Maybe I better go see.

CROOKS

more gently: I didn't mean to scare you. He'll come back. I was talkin' about myself.

LENNIE

miserably: George won't go away and leave me. I know George won't do that.

CROOKS

continuing dreamily: I remember when I was a little kid on my ole man's chicken ranch. Had two brothers. They was always near me, always there. Used to sleep right in the same room. Right in the same bed, all three. Had a strawberry patch. Had an alfalfa patch. Used to turn the chickens out in the alfalfa on a sunny morning. Me and my brothers would set on the fence and watch 'em—white chickens they was.

LENNIE

interested: George says we're gonna have alfalfa.

CROOKS:

You're nuts.

LENNIE:

We are too gonna get it. You ask George.

CROOKS

scornfully: You're nuts. I seen hundreds of men come by on the road and on the ranches, bindles on their back and that same damn thing in their head. Hundreds of 'em. They come and they quit and they go on. And every damn one of 'em is got a little piece of land in his head. And never a goddamn one of 'em gets it. Jus' like heaven. Everybody wants a little piece of land. Nobody never gets to heaven. And nobody gets no land.

LENNIE:

We are too.

CROOKS:

It's jest in your head. Guys all the time talkin' about it, but it's jest in your head. *The horses move restlessly. One of them whinnies.* I guess somebody's out there.

Maybe Slim. *Pulls himself painfully upright and moves toward the door. Calls:* That you, Slim?

CANDY

from outside: Slim went in town. Say, you seen Lennie?

CROOKS:

You mean the big guy?

CANDY:

Yes. Seen him around any place?

CROOKS

goes back to his bunk and sits down, says shortly: He's in here.

CANDY

stands in the doorway, scratching his wrist. Makes no attempt to enter: Look, Lennie, I been figuring something out. About the place.

CROOKS

irritably: You can come in if you want.

CANDY

embarrassed: I don't know. Course if you want me to.

CROOKS:

Oh, come on in. Everybody's comin' in. You might just as well. Gettin' to be a goddamn race track. *He tries to conceal his pleasure.*

CANDY

still embarrassed: You've got a nice cozy little place in here. Must be nice to have a room to yourself this way.

CROOKS:

Sure. And a manure pile under the window. All to myself. It's swell.

LENNIE

breaking in: You said about the place.

CANDY:

You know, I been here a long time. An' Crooks been here a long time. This is the first time I ever been in his room.

CROOKS

darkly: Guys don't come in a colored man's room. Nobody been here but Slim.

LENNIE

insistently: The place. You said about the place.

CANDY:

Yeah. I got it all figured out. We can make some real money on them rabbits if we go about it right.

LENNIE:

But I get to tend 'em. George says I get to tend 'em. He promised.

128

CROOKS

brutally: You guys is just kiddin' yourselves. You'll talk about it a hell of a lot, but you won't get no land. You'll be a swamper here until they take you out in a box. Hell, I seen too many guys.

CANDY

angrily: We're gonna do it. George says we are. We got the money right now.

CROOKS:

Yeah. And where is George now? In town in a whore-house. That's where your money's goin'. I tell you I seen it happen too many times.

CANDY:

George ain't got the money in town. The money's in the bank. Me and Lennie and George. We gonna have a room to ourselves. We gonna have a dog and chickens. We gonna have green corn and maybe a cow.

CROOKS

impressed: You say you got the money?

CANDY:

We got most of it. Just a little bit more to get. Have it all in one month. George's got the land all picked out too.

CROOKS

exploring his spine with his hands: I've never seen a guy really do it. I seen guys nearly crazy with loneliness for land, but every time a whorehouse or a blackjack game took it away from 'em. *Hesitates and then speaks timidly:* If you guys would want a hand to work for nothin'—just his keep, why I'd come and lend a hand. I ain't so crippled I can't work like a son-of-a-bitch if I wanted to.

GEORGE

strolls through the door, hands in pockets, leans against the wall, speaks in a half-satiric, rather gentle voice: You couldn't go to bed like I told you, could you, Lennie? Hell, no—you got to get out in society an' flap your mouth. Holdin' a convention out here.

LENNIE

defending himself: You was gone. There wasn't nobody in the bunkhouse. I ain't done no bad things, George.

GEORGE

still casually: Only time I get any peace is when you're asleep. If you ever get walkin' in your sleep I'll chop off your head like a chicken. *Chops with his hand.*

130

CROOKS

coming to Lennie's defense: We was jus' settin' here talkin'. Ain't no harm in that.

GEORGE:

Yeah. I heard you. *A weariness has settled on him.* Got to be here ever' minute, I guess. Got to watch ya. *To Crooks:* It ain't nothing against you, Crooks. We just wasn't gonna tell nobody.

CANDY

tries to change subject: Didn't you have no fun in town?

GEORGE:

Oh! I set in a chair and Susy was crackin' jokes an' the guys was startin' to raise a little puny hell. Christ Almighty—I never been this way before. I'm jus' gonna set out a dime and a nickel for a shot an' I think what a hell of a lot of bulk carrot seed you can get for fifteen cents.

CANDY:

Not in them damn little envelopes—but bulk seed—you sure can.

GEORGE:

So purty soon I come back. I can't think of nothing else. Them guys slingin' money around got me jumpy.

CANDY:

Guy got to have *some* fun. I was to a parlor house in Bakersfield once. God Almighty, what a place. Went upstairs on a red carpet. They was big pitchers on the wall. We set in big sof' chairs. They was cigarettes on the table—an' they was *free.* Purty soon a Jap come in with drinks on a tray an' them *drinks* was free. Take all you want. *In a reverie:* Purty soon the girls come in an' they was jus' as polite an' nice an' quiet an' purty. Didn't seem like hookers. Made ya kinda scared to ask 'em. . . . That was a long time ago.

GEORGE:

Yeah? An' what'd them sof' chairs set you back?

CANDY:

Fifteen bucks.

GEORGE

scornfully: So ya got a cigarette an' a whiskey an' a look at a purty dress an' it cost ya twelve and a half bucks extra. You shot a week's pay to walk on that red carpet.

CANDY

still entranced with his memory: A week's pay? Sure. But I worked weeks all my life. I can't remember none of them weeks. But . . . that was nearly twenty years

132

ago. And I can remember that. Girl I went with was named Arline. Had on a pink silk dress.

GEORGE

turns suddenly and looks out the door into the dark barn, speaks savagely: I s'pose ya lookin' for Curley? *Curley's Wife appears in the door.* Well, Curley ain't here.

CURLEY'S WIFE

determined now: I know Curley ain't here. I wanted to ast Crooks somepin'. I didn't know you guys was here.

CANDY:

Didn't George tell you before—we don't want nothing to do with you. You know damn well Curley ain't here.

CURLEY'S WIFE:

I know where Curley went. Got his arm in a sling an' he went anyhow. I tell ya I come out to ast Crooks somepin.'

CROOKS

apprehensively: Maybe you better go along to your own house. You hadn't ought to come near a colored man's room. I don't want no trouble. You don't want to ask me nothing.

133

CANDY

rubbing his wrist stump: You got a husband. You got no call to come foolin' around with other guys, causin' trouble.

CURLEY'S WIFE

suddenly angry: I try to be nice an' polite to you lousy bindle bums—but you're too good. I tell ya I could of went with shows. An'—an' a guy wanted to put me in pitchers right in Hollywood. *Looks about to see how she is impressing them. Their eyes are hard.* I come out here to ast somebody somepin' an'——

CANDY

stands up suddenly and knocks his nail keg over backward, speaks angrily: I had enough. You ain't wanted here. We tole you, you ain't. Callin' us bindle stiffs. You got floozy idears what us guys amounts to. You ain't got sense enough to see us guys ain't bindle stiffs. S'pose you could get us *canned*—s'pose you *could.* You think we'd hit the highway an' look for another two-bit job. You don't know we got our own ranch to go to an' our own house an' fruit trees. An' we got friends. That's what we got. Maybe they was a time when we didn't have nothing, but that ain't so no more.

CURLEY'S WIFE:

You damn ol' goat. If you had two bits, you'd be in Soledad gettin' a drink an' suckin' the bottom of the glass.

GEORGE:

Maybe she could ask Crooks what she come to ask an' then get the hell home. I don't think she come to ask nothing.

CURLEY'S WIFE:

What happened to Curley's hand? *Crooks laughs. George tries to shut him up.* So it wasn't no machine. Curley didn't act like he was tellin' the truth. Come on, Crooks—what happened?

CROOKS:

I wasn't there. I didn't see it.

CURLEY'S WIFE:

eagerly: What happened? I won't let on to Curley. He says he caught his han' in a gear. *Crooks is silent.* Who done it?

GEORGE:

Didn't nobody do it.

CURLEY'S WIFE

turns slowly to George: So *you* done it. Well, he had it comin'.

Of Mice and Men

GEORGE:

I didn't have no fuss with Curley.

CURLEY'S WIFE

steps near him, smiling: Maybe now you ain't scared of him no more. Maybe you'll talk to me sometimes now. Ever'body was scared of him.

GEORGE

speaks rather kindly: Look! I didn't sock Curley. If he had trouble, it ain't none of our affair. Ask Curley about it. Now listen. I'm gonna try to tell ya. We tole you to get the hell out and it don't do no good. So I'm gonna tell you another way. Us guys got somepin' we're gonna do. If you stick around you'll gum up the works. It ain't your fault. If a guy steps on a round pebble an' falls down an' breaks his neck, it ain't the pebble's fault, but the guy wouldn't of did it if the pebble wasn't there.

CURLEY'S WIFE

puzzled: What you talkin' about pebbles? If you didn't sock Curley, who did? *She looks at the others, then steps quickly over to Lennie.* Where'd you get them bruises on your face?

GEORGE:

I tell you he got his hand caught in a machine.

136

LENNIE

looks anxiously at George, speaks miserably: He caught his han' in a machine.

GEORGE:

So now get out of here.

CURLEY'S WIFE

goes close to Lennie, speaks softly and there is a note of affection in her voice: So . . . it was you. Well . . . maybe you're dumb like they say . . . an' maybe . . . you're the only guy on the ranch with guts. *She puts her hand on Lennie's shoulder. He looks up in her face and a smile grows on his face. She strokes his shoulder.* You're a nice fella.

GEORGE

suddenly leaps at her ferociously, grabs her shoulder and whirls her around: Listen . . . you! I tried to give you a break. Don't you walk into nothing! We ain't gonna let you mess up what we're gonna do. You let this guy alone an' get the hell out of here.

CURLEY'S WIFE

defiant but slightly frightened: You ain't tellin' me what to do. *The Boss appears in the door, stands legs spread, thumbs hooked over his belt.* I got a right to talk to anybody I want to.

GEORGE

Why, you—— *George, furious, steps close—his hand is raised to strike her. She cowers a little. George stiffens, seeing Boss, frozen in position. The others see Boss too. Girl retreats slowly. George's hand drops slowly to his side—he takes two slow backward steps. Hold the scene for a moment.*

CURTAIN

ACT THREE

ACT THREE: SCENE I

Mid-afternoon Sunday.

One end of a great barn. Backstage the hay slopes up sharply against the wall. High in the upstage wall is a large hay window. On each side are seen the hay racks, behind which are the stalls with the horses in them. Throughout this scene the horses can be heard in their stalls, rattling their halter chains and chewing at the hay.

The entrance is downstage right.

The boards of the barn are not close together. Streaks of afternoon sun come between the boards, made visible by dust in the air. From outside comes the clang of horseshoes on the playing peg, shouts of men encouraging or jeering.

In the barn there is a feeling of quiet and humming and lazy warmth. Curtain rises on Lennie sitting in the hay, looking down at a little dead puppy in front of him. He puts out his big hand and strokes it clear from one end to the other.

LENNIE

softly: Why do you got to get killed? You ain't so little as mice. I didn' bounce you hard. *Bends the pup's head up and looks in its face.* Now maybe George ain't gonna let me tend no rabbits if he finds out you got killed. *He scoops a little hollow and lays the puppy in it out of sight and covers it over with hay. He stares at the mound he has made.* This ain't no bad thing like I got to hide in the brush. I'll tell George I found it dead. *He unburies the pup and inspects it. Twists its ears and works his fingers in its fur. Sorrowfully:* But he'll know. George always knows. He'll say: "You done it. Don't try to put nothin' over on me." And he'll say: "Now just for that you don't get to tend no—you-know-whats." *His anger rises. Addresses the pup:* God damn you. Why do you got to get killed? You ain't so little as mice. *Picks up the pup and hurls it from him and turns his back on it. He sits bent over his knees moaning to himself:* Now he won't let me. . . . Now he won't let me. *Outside there is a clang of horseshoes on the iron stake and a little chorus of cries. Lennie gets up and brings the pup back and lays it in the hay and sits down. He mourns:* You wasn't big enough. They tole me and tole me you wasn't. I didn't know you'd get killed so easy.

142

Maybe George won't care. This here goddamn little son-of-a-bitch wasn't nothin' to George.

CANDY

voice from behind the stalls: Lennie, where you at? *Lennie frantically buries the pup under the hay. Candy enters excitedly.* Thought I'd find ya here. Say . . . I been talkin' to Slim. It's okay. We ain't gonna get the can. Slim been talkin' to the boss. Slim tol' the boss you guys is good buckers. The boss got to move that grain. 'Member what hell the boss give us las' night? He tol' Slim he got his eye on you an' George. But you ain't gonna get the can. Oh! an' say. The boss give Curley's wife hell, too. Tole her never to go near the men no more. Give her worse hell than you an' George. *For the first time notices Lennie's dejection.* Ain't you glad?

LENNIE:

Sure.

CANDY:

You ain't sick?

LENNIE:

Uh-uh!

CANDY:

I got to go tell George. See you later. *Exits.*

Lennie, alone, uncovers the pup. Lies down in the hay

*and sinks deep in it. Puts the pup on his arm and
strokes it. Curley's Wife enters secretly. A little mound
of hay conceals Lennie from her. In her hand she carries a small suitcase, very cheap. She crosses the barn
and buries the case in the hay. Stands up and looks to
see whether it can be seen. Lennie watching her quietly
tries to cover the pup with hay. She sees the move-
ment.*

CURLEY'S WIFE:

What—what you doin' here?

LENNIE

sullenly: Jus' settin' here.

CURLEY'S WIFE:

You seen what I done.

LENNIE:

Yeah! you brang a valise.

CURLEY'S WIFE

comes near to him: You won't tell—will you?

LENNIE

still sullen: I ain't gonna have nothing to do with you.
George tole me. I ain't to talk to you or nothing. *Covers the pup a little more.*

CURLEY'S WIFE:

George give you all your orders?

LENNIE:

Not talk nor nothing.

CURLEY'S WIFE:

You won't tell about that suitcase? I ain't gonna stay here no more. Tonight I'm gonna get out. Come here an' get my stuff an' get out. I ain't gonna be run over no more. I'm gonna go in pitchers. *Sees Lennie's hand stroking the pup under the hay.* What you got there?

LENNIE:

Nuthing. I ain't gonna talk to you. George says I ain't.

CURLEY'S WIFE:

Listen: The guys got a horseshoe tenement out there. It's on'y four o'clock. Them guys ain't gonna leave that tenement. They got money bet. You don't need to be scared to talk to me.

LENNIE

weakening a little: I ain't supposed to.

CURLEY'S WIFE

watching his buried hand: What you got under there?

LENNIE

his woe comes back to him: Jus' my pup. Jus' my little ol' pup. *Sweeps the hay aside.*

CURLEY'S WIFE:

Why! He's dead.

LENNIE

explaining sadly: He was so little. I was jus' playin' with him—an' he made like he's gonna bite me—an' I made like I'm gonna smack him—an'—I done it. An' then he was dead.

CURLEY'S WIFE

consolingly: Don't you worry none. He was just a mutt. The whole country is full of mutts.

LENNIE:

It ain't that so much. George gonna be mad. Maybe he won't let me—what he said I could tend.

CURLEY'S WIFE

sits down in the hay beside him, speaks soothingly: Don't you worry. Them guys got money bet on that horseshoe tenement. They ain't gonna leave it. And tomorra I'll be gone. I ain't gonna let them run over me.

In the following scene it is apparent that neither is listening to the other and yet as it goes on, as a happy tone increases, it can be seen that they are growing closer together.

LENNIE:

We gonna have a little place an' raspberry bushes.

146

CURLEY'S WIFE:

I ain't meant to live like this. I come from Salinas. Well, a show come through an' I talked to a guy that was in it. He says I could go with the show. My ol' lady wouldn' let me, 'cause I was on'y fifteen. I wouldn't be no place like this if I had went with that show, you bet.

LENNIE:

Gonna take a sack an' fill it up with alfalfa an'——

CURLEY'S WIFE

hurrying on: 'Nother time I met a guy an' he was in pitchers. Went out to the Riverside Dance Palace with him. He said he was gonna put me in pitchers. Says I was a natural. Soon's he got back to Hollywood he was gonna write me about it. *Looks impressively at Lennie.* I never got that letter. I think my ol' lady stole it. Well, I wasn't gonna stay no place where they stole your letters. So I married Curley. Met *him* out to the Riverside Dance Palace too.

LENNIE:

I hope George ain't gonna be mad about this pup.

CURLEY'S WIFE:

I ain't tol' this to nobody before. Maybe I oughtn' to.

147

I don't like Curley. He ain't a nice fella. I might a stayed with him but last night him an' his ol' man both lit into me. I don't have to stay here. *Moves closer and speaks confidentially:* Don't tell nobody till I get clear away. I'll go in the night an' thumb a ride to Hollywood.

LENNIE:

We gonna get out a here purty soon. This ain't no nice place.

CURLEY'S WIFE

ecstatically: Gonna get in the movies an' have nice clothes—all them nice clothes like they wear. An' I'll set in them big hotels and they'll take pitchers of me. When they have them openings I'll go an' talk in the radio . . . an' it won't cost me nothing 'cause I'm in the pitcher. *Puts her hand on Lennie's arm for a moment.* All them nice clothes like they wear . . . because this guy says I'm a natural.

LENNIE:

We gonna go way . . . far away from here.

CURLEY'S WIFE:

'Course, when I run away from Curley, my ol' lady won't never speak to me no more. She'll think I ain't decent. That's what she'll say. *Defiantly:* Well, we

148

really ain't decent, no matter how much my ol' lady tries to hide it, My ol' man was a drunk. They put him away. There! Now I told.

LENNIE:

George an' me was to the Sacramento Fair. One time I fell in the river an' George pulled me out an' saved me, an' then we went to the Fair. They got all kinds of stuff there. We seen long-hair rabbits.

CURLEY'S WIFE:

My ol' man was a sign-painter when he worked. He used to get drunk an' paint crazy pitchers an' waste paint. One night when I was a little kid, him an' my ol' lady had an awful fight. They was always fightin'. In the middle of the night he come into my room, and he says, "I can't stand this no more. Let's you an' me go away." I guess he was drunk. *Her voice takes on a curious wondering tenderness:* I remember in the night—walkin' down the road, and the trees was black. I was pretty sleepy. He picked me up, an' he carried me on his back. He says, "We gonna live to- gether. We gonna live together because you're my own little girl, an' not no stranger. No arguin' and fightin'," he says, "because you're my little daughter." *Her voice becomes soft:* He says, "Why you'll bake little cakes for me, an' I'll paint pretty pitchers all over the wall." *Sadly:* In the morning they caught us . . . an' they put him away. *Pause.* I wish we'd a' went.

LENNIE:

Maybe if I took this here pup an' throwed him away George wouldn't never know.

CURLEY'S WIFE:

They locked him up for a drunk, and in a little while he died.

LENNIE:

Then maybe I could tend the rabbits without no trouble.

CURLEY'S WIFE:

Don't you think of nothing but rabbits? *Sound of horseshoe on metal.* Somebody made a ringer.

LENNIE

patiently: We gonna have a house and a garden, an' a place for alfalfa. And I take a sack and get it all full of alfalfa, and then I take it to the rabbits.

CURLEY'S WIFE:

What makes you so nuts about rabbits?

LENNIE

moves close to her: I like to pet nice things. Once at a fair I seen some of them long-hair rabbits. And they was nice, you bet. *Despairingly:* I'd even pet mice, but not when I could get nothin' better.

CURLEY'S WIFE

giggles: I think you're nuts.

LENNIE

earnestly: No, I ain't. George says I ain't. I like to pet nice things with my fingers. Soft things.

CURLEY'S WIFE:

Well, who don't? Everybody likes that. I like to feel silk and velvet. You like to feel velvet?

LENNIE

chuckling with pleasure: You bet, by God. And I had some too. A lady give me some. And that lady was— my Aunt Clara. She give it right to me. . . . *Measuring with his hands:* 'Bout this big a piece. I wisht I had that velvet right now. *He frowns.* I lost it. I ain't seen it for a long time.

CURLEY'S WIFE

laughing: You're nuts. But you're a kinda nice fella. Jus' like a big baby. A person can see kinda what you mean. When I'm doin' my hair sometimes I jus' set there and stroke it, because it's so soft. *Runs her fingers over the top of her head.* Some people got kinda coarse hair. You take Curley, his hair's just like wire. But

151

mine is soft and fine. Here, feel. Right here. *Takes Lennie's hand and puts it on her head.* Feel there and see how soft it is. *Lennie's fingers fall to stroking her hair.* Don't you muss it up.

LENNIE:

Oh, that's nice. *Strokes harder.* Oh, that's nice.

CURLEY'S WIFE:

Look out now, you'll muss it. *Angrily:* You stop it now, you'll mess it all up. *She jerks her head sideways and Lennie's fingers close on her hair and hang on. In a panic:* Let go. *She screams:* You let go. *She screams again. His other hand closes over her mouth and nose.*

LENNIE

begging: Oh, please don't do that. George'll be mad. *She struggles violently to be free. A soft screaming comes from under Lennie's hand. Crying with fright:* Oh, please don't do none of that. George gonna say I done a bad thing. *He raises his hand from her mouth and a hoarse cry escapes. Angrily:* Now don't. I don't want you to yell. You gonna get me in trouble just like George says you will. Now don't you do that. *She struggles more.* Don't you go yellin'. *He shakes her violently. Her neck snaps sideways and she lies still. Looks down at her and cautiously removes his hand from over her mouth.* I don't wanta hurt you. But George will be mad if you yell. *When she doesn't answer he bends closely over her. He lifts her arm and lets it drop. For a moment he seems bewildered.* I done a bad thing. I done another bad thing. *He paws up the hay until it partly covers her. The sound of the horseshoe game comes from the outside. And for the first time Lennie seems conscious of it. He crouches down and listens.* Oh, I done a real bad thing. I shouldn't a did that. George will be mad. And . . . he said . . . and hide in the brush till he comes. . . . He's gonna be mad . . . in the brush till he comes. That's what he said. *He picks up the puppy from beside the girl.* I'll throw him away. It's bad enough like it is.

He puts the pup under his coat, creeps to the barn wall and peers out between the cracks and then he creeps around to the end of the manger and disappears. The stage is vacant except for Curley's Wife. She lies in the hay half covered up and she looks very young and peaceful. Her rouged cheeks and red lips make her seem alive and sleeping lightly. For a moment the stage is absolutely silent. Then the horses stamp on the other side of the feeding rack. The halter chains clink and from outside men's voices come loud and clear.

CANDY

offstage: Lennie! Oh, Lennie, you in there? *He enters.* I been figurin' some more, Lennie. Tell you what we can do. *Sees Curley's Wife and stops. Rubs his white whiskers.* I didn't know you was here. You was tol' not to be here. *He steps near her.* You oughtn't to sleep out here. *He is right beside her and looks down.* Oh, Jesus Christ! *Goes to the door and calls softly:* George, George! Come here . . . George!

GEORGE

enters: What do you want?

CANDY

points at Curley's Wife: Look.

GEORGE:

What's the matter with her? *Steps up beside her.* Oh, Jesus Christ!

Kneels beside her and feels her heart and her wrist. Finally stands up slowly and stiffly. From this time on through the rest of the scene George is wooden.

CANDY:

What done it?

GEORGE

coldly: Ain't you got any idea? *Candy looks away.* I should of knew. I guess way back in my head I did.

CANDY:

What we gonna do now, George? What we gonna do now?

GEORGE

answering slowly and dully: Guess . . . we gotta . . . tell . . . the guys. Guess we got to catch him and lock him up. We can't let him get away. Why, the poor bastard would starve. *He tries to reassure himself.* Maybe they'll lock him up and be nice to him.

CANDY

excitedly: You know better'n that, George. You know Curley's gonna want to get him lynched. You know how Curley is.

GEORGE:

Yeah. . . . Yeah . . . that's right. I know Curley. And the other guys too. *He looks back at Curley's Wife.*

CANDY

pleadingly: You and me can get that little place can't we, George? You and me can go there and live nice, can't we? Can't we? *Candy drops his head and looks down at the hay to indicate that he knows.*

GEORGE

shakes his head slowly: It was somethin' me and him had. *Softly:* I think I knowed it from the very first. I think I knowed we'd never do her. He used to like to hear about it so much. I got fooled to thinkin' maybe we would. *Candy starts to speak but doesn't.*

GEORGE

as though repeating a lesson: I'll work my month and then I'll take my fifty bucks. I'll stay all night in some lousy cat-house or I'll set in a pool room until every-body goes home. An' then—I'll come back an' work another month. And then I'll have fifty bucks more.

CANDY:

He's such a nice fellow. I didn't think he'd a done nothing like this.

GEORGE

gets a grip on himself and straightens his shoulders: Now listen. We gotta tell the guys. I guess they've gotta bring him in. They ain't no way out. Maybe they won't hurt him. I ain't gonna let 'em hurt Lennie. *Sharply:* Now you listen. The guys might think I was in on it. I'm gonna go in the bunkhouse. Then in a minute you come out and yell like you just seen her. Will you do that? So the guys won't think I was in on it?

156

CANDY:

Sure, George. Sure, I'll do that.

GEORGE:

Okay. Give me a couple of minutes then. And then you yell your head off. I'm goin' now. *George exits.*

CANDY

watches him go, looks helplessly back at Curley's Wife; his next words are in sorrow and in anger: You goddamn tramp. You done it, didn't you? Everybody knowed you'd mess things up. You just wasn't no good. *His voice shakes:* I could of hoed in the garden and washed dishes for them guys. . . . *Pauses for a moment and then goes into a sing-song repeating the old words:* If there was a circus or a baseball game . . . we would o' went to her . . . just said to hell with work and went to her. And they'd been a pig and chickens . . . and in the winter a little fat stove. An' us jus' settin' there . . . settin' there. . . . *His eyes blind with tears and he goes weakly to the entrance of the barn. Tries for a moment to break a shout out of his throat before he succeeds.* Hey, you guys! Come here! Come here!

Outside the noise of the horseshoe game stops. The sound of discussion and then the voices come closer:

"What's the matter?" . . . *"Who's that?"* . . . *"It's Candy."* . . . *"Something must have happened."*

Enter Slim and Carlson, Young Whit and Curley, Crooks in the back, keeping out of attention range. And last of all George. George has put on his blue denim coat and buttoned it. His black hat is pulled down low over his eyes.

"What's the matter?" . . . *"What's happened?"*

A gesture from Candy.

The men stare at Curley's Wife. Slim goes over to her, feels her wrist and touches her cheek with his fingers. His hand goes under her slightly twisted neck.

Curley comes near. For a moment he seems shocked. Looks around helplessly and suddenly he comes to life.

CURLEY:

I know who done it. That big son-of-a-bitch done it. I know he done it. Why, everybody else was out there playing horseshoes. *Working himself into a fury:* I'm gonna get him. I'm gonna get my shotgun. Why, I'll kill the big son-of-a-bitch myself. I'll shoot him in the guts. Come on, you guys. *He runs out of the barn.*

CARLSON:

I'll go get my Luger. *He runs out too.*

158

SLIM

quietly to George: I guess Lennie done it all right. Her neck's busted. Lennie could o' did that. *George nods slowly. Half-questioning:* Maybe like that time in Weed you was tellin' me about. *George nods. Gently:* Well. I guess we got to get him. Where you think he might o' went?

GEORGE

struggling to get words out: I don't know.

SLIM:

I guess we gotta get him.

GEORGE

stepping close and speaking passionately: Couldn't we maybe bring him in and lock him up? He's nuts, Slim, he never done this to be mean.

SLIM:

If we could only keep Curley in. But Curley wants to shoot him. *He thinks.* And s'pose they lock him up, George, and strap him down and put him in a cage, that ain't no good.

GEORGE:

I know. I know.

SLIM:

I think there's only one way to get him out of it.

159

GEORGE:

I know.

CARLSON

enters running: The bastard stole my Luger. It ain't in my bag.

CURLEY

enters carrying a shotgun in his good hand. Officiously: All right, you guys. The nigger's got a shotgun. You take it, Carlson.

WHIT:

Only cover around here is down by the river. He might have went there.

CURLEY:

Don't give him no chance. Shoot for his guts, that'll double him over.

WHIT:

I ain't got a gun.

CURLEY:

Go in and tell my old man. Get a gun from him. Let's go now. *Turns suspiciously on George:* You're comin' with us, fella!

GEORGE:

Yeah. I'll come. But listen, Curley, the poor bastard's nuts. Don't shoot him, he didn't know what he was doin'.

160

CURLEY:

Don't shoot him! He's got Carlson's Luger, ain't he?

GEORGE

weakly: Maybe Carlson lost his gun.

CARLSON:

I seen it this morning. It's been took.

SLIM

looking down at Curley's Wife: Curley, maybe you better stay here with your wife. *The light is fading into evening. Curley hesitates. Seems almost to weaken, then he hardens again.*

CURLEY:

Naw, I'm gonna shoot the guts out of that big bastard, I'm gonna get him myself. Come on, you guys.

SLIM

to Candy: You stay here then, Candy. The rest of us better get goin'. *They walk out, Slim and George last. Exeunt all but Candy. He squats in the hay, watching the face of Curley's Wife.*

CANDY:

Poor bastard.

CURTAIN

ACT THREE: SCENE II

Evening.

The river bank again.

Light from the setting sun shines on the low brown hills. Among the trees by the river, the shade is deep with evening feeling.

Sounds: distant barking of dogs and the quiet call of quail.

The curtain rises on an empty stage.

There is a sudden whistle of evening wind that stirs the trees and scuds the leaves on the ground.

The stage is still again. Lennie enters as silently as a bear. He is bent over and wary. On stage he looks behind him. Then he takes from under his coat the dead pup, lays it on the ground and, going to the river, lies on his stomach and drinks.

He returns to the dead pup, sits down beside it.

LENNIE:

George gonna give me hell . . . I bet. I . . . won't

162

tell him. I'll bury him. *Begins to scoop a hole in the sand in front of him. Softly:* But I didn't forget, you bet. I come right here. Hide in the brush an' wait for George. *Works carefully at his little grave, shaping the hole. At last he picks up the pup and lays it in the hole. Mourning:* He gonna give me hell. He gonna wish he was alone. *Adjusts the puppy in the hole, turning it around to make it fit better. Defiantly:* Well . . . I can go right up in the hills an' find a cave. 'Course I wouldn't never have no ketchup. *Begins packing sand down carefully about the pup, patting it as he does in beat with his words.* I'll—go—away—go—away. *Every word a pat. Fills the grave carefully, smooths the sand over it.* There now. *Gathers leaves and scatters them over the place. Gets up on his knees and cocks his head to inspect the job.* Now. I won't never tell George. *Sinks back to a sitting position.* He'll know. He always knows.

Far off sound of voices approaching. They come closer during the scene. Suddenly there is the clicking warning of a cock-quail and then the drum of the flock's wings. George enters silently, but hurriedly.

GEORGE

in a hoarse whisper: Get in the tules—quick.

LENNIE:

I ain't done nothing, George. *The voices are very close.*

GEORGE

frantically: Get in the tules—damn you. *Voices are nearly there. George half pushes Lennie down among the tules. The tops rustle showing his crawling progress.*

WHIT

offstage: There's George. *Enters.* Better not get so far ahead. You ain't got a gun. *Enter Slim, Carlson, Boss, Curley, and three other ranch hands. They are armed with shotguns and rifles.*

CARLSON:

He musta come this way. Them prints in the sand was aimed this way.

SLIM

has been regarding George: Now look. We ain't gonna find him stickin' in a bunch this way. We got to spread out.

CURLEY:

Brush is pretty thick here. He might be lying in the brush. *Steps toward the tules. George moves quickly after him.*

SLIM

Seeing the move speaks quickly: Look—*pointing*—up there's the county road an' open fields an' over there's the highway. Le's spread out an' cover the brush.

BOSS:

Slim's right. We got to spread.

SLIM:

We better drag up to the roads an' then drag back.

CURLEY:

'Member what I said—shoot for his guts.

SLIM:

Okay, move out. Me an' George'll go up to the county road. You guys gets the highway an' drag back.

BOSS:

If we get separated, we'll meet here. Remember this place.

CURLEY:

All I care is getting the bastard. *The men move off-stage right, talking. Slim and George move slowly up-stage listening to the voices that grow fainter and fainter.*

SLIM

softly to George: Where is he? *George looks at him in*

165

Of *Mice and Men*

the eyes for a long moment. Finally trusts him and points with his thumb toward the tules.

SLIM:

You want—I should—go away?

George nods slowly, looking at the ground. Slim starts away, comes back, tries to say something, instead puts his hand on George's shoulder for a second, and then hurries off upstage.

GEORGE

Moves woodenly toward the bank and the tule clump and sits down: Lennie! *The tules shiver again and Lennie emerges dripping.*

LENNIE:

Where's them guys goin'? *Long pause.*

GEORGE:

Huntin'.

LENNIE:

Whyn't we go with 'em? I like huntin'. *Waits for an answer. George stares across the river.* Is it 'cause I done a bad thing?

GEORGE:

It don't make no difference.

LENNIE:

Is that why we can't go huntin' with them guys?

166

GEORGE

woodenly: It don't make no difference. . . . Sit down, Lennie. Right there. *The light is going now. In the distance there are shouts of men. George turns his head and listens to the shouts.*

LENNIE:

George!

GEORGE:

Yeah?

LENNIE:

Ain't you gonna give me hell?

GEORGE:

Give ya hell?

LENNIE:

Sure. . . . Like you always done before. Like—"If I didn' have you I'd take my fifty bucks . . ."

GEORGE

softly as if in wonder: Jesus Christ, Lennie, you can't remember nothing that happens. But you remember every word I say!

LENNIE:

Well, ain't you gonna say it?

GEORGE

reciting: "If I was alone I—could live—so easy. *His*

167

voice is monotonous. I could get a job and not have no mess. . . ."

LENNIE:

Go on, go on! "And when the end of the month come . . ."

GEORGE:

"And when the end of the month come, I could take my fifty bucks and go to—a cat-house. . . ."

LENNIE

eagerly: Go on, George, ain't you gonna give me no more hell?

GEORGE:

No!

LENNIE:

I can go away. I'll go right off in the hills and find a cave if you don't want me.

GEORGE

speaks as though his lips were stiff: No, I want you to stay here with me.

LENNIE

craftily: Then tell me like you done before.

GEORGE:

Tell you what?

LENNIE:

’Bout the other guys and about us!

GEORGE

recites again: “Guys like us got no families. They got a little stake and then they blow it in. They ain’t got nobody in the world that gives a hoot in hell about ’em!”

LENNIE

happily: “But not *us*.” Tell about us now.

GEORGE:

“But not us.”

LENNIE:

“Because . . .”

GEORGE:

“Because I got you and . . .”

LENNIE

triumphantly: “And I got you. We got each other,” that’s what, that gives a hoot in hell about us. *A breeze blows up the leaves and then they settle back again. There are the shouts of men again. This time closer.*

GEORGE

takes off his hat; shakily: Take off your hat, Lennie. The air feels fine!

LENNIE

removes his hat and lays it on the ground in front of him: Tell how it's gonna be. *Again the sound of men. George listens to them.*

GEORGE:

Look acrost the river, Lennie, and I'll tell you like you can almost see it. *Lennie turns his head and looks across the river.* "We gonna get a little place . . . *Reaches in his side pocket and brings out Carlson's Luger. Hand and gun lie on the ground behind Lennie's back. He stares at the back of Lennie's head at the place where spine and skull are joined. Sounds of men's voices talking offstage.*

LENNIE:

Go on! *George raises the gun, but his hand shakes and he drops his hand on to the ground.* Go on! How's it gonna be? "We gonna get a little place. . . ."

GEORGE

thickly: "We'll have a cow. And we'll have maybe a pig and chickens—and down the flat we'll have a . . . little piece of alfalfa. . . ."

LENNIE

shouting: "For the rabbits!"

170

GEORGE:

"For the rabbits!"

LENNIE:

"And I get to tend the rabbits?"

GEORGE:

"And you get to tend the rabbits!"

LENNIE

giggling with happiness: "And live on the fat o' the land!"

GEORGE:

Yes. *Lennie turns his head. Quickly:* Look over there, Lennie. Like you can really see it.

LENNIE:

Where?

GEORGE:

Right acrost that river there. Can't you almost see it?

LENNIE

moving: Where, George?

GEORGE:

It's over there. You keep lookin', Lennie. Just keep lookin'.

LENNIE:

I'm lookin', George. I'm lookin'.

Of Mice and Men

GEORGE:

That's right. It's gonna be nice there. Ain't gonna be no trouble, no fights. Nobody ever gonna hurt nobody, or steal from 'em. It's gonna be—nice.

LENNIE:

I can see it, George. I can see it! Right over there! I can see it! *George fires. Lennie crumples; falls behind the brush. The voices of the men in the distance.*

CURTAIN